I sat forward. "What can you tell me about Halaquez?"

The madam was frowning. "That he was a patron here. That he's a ruthless killer with sadistic tastes that bleed over into his sexual kinks. His needs extend well beyond what we provide here at Mandor."

"It's a way to find him. You must know other houses or girls working solo, doing the S & M thing."

Bunny's eyes were tight. "I think you will find Mr. Halaquez is banned from all such establishments. But I will give you a list, if you think that may help."

"It's a start."

"The only other thing…but it's a long shot."

"Hell. Guys get rich playing long shots. Go."

Again she chose her words carefully. "There is a rumor… and for now it's just a rumor…that the Consummata is setting up shop in Miami."

I blinked. "Who or what is the 'Consummata'?"

"A very famous dominatrix."

"From Miami?"

"From nowhere. From everywhere. Her clients, they say, are among the most rich and powerful men. She is a rumor. A wisp of smoke. A legend. If Jaimie Halaquez hears that the Consummata has graced Miami with her presence, he won't be able to resist…"

**SOME OTHER HARD CASE CRIME BOOKS
YOU WILL ENJOY:**

DEAD STREET *by Mickey Spillane*
THE FIRST QUARRY *by Max Allan Collins*
THE LAST QUARRY *by Max Allan Collins*
QUARRY IN THE MIDDLE *by Max Allan Collins*
QUARRY'S EX *by Max Allan Collins*
TWO FOR THE MONEY *by Max Allan Collins*
DEADLY BELOVED *by Max Allan Collins*

FIFTY-TO-ONE *by Charles Ardai*
KILLING CASTRO *by Lawrence Block*
THE DEAD MAN'S BROTHER *by Roger Zelazny*
THE CUTIE *by Donald E. Westlake*
HOUSE DICK *by E. Howard Hunt*
CASINO MOON *by Peter Blauner*
FAKE I.D. *by Jason Starr*
PASSPORT TO PERIL *by Robert B. Parker*
STOP THIS MAN! *by Peter Rabe*
LOSERS LIVE LONGER *by Russell Atwood*
HONEY IN HIS MOUTH *by Lester Dent*
THE CORPSE WORE PASTIES *by Jonny Porkpie*
THE VALLEY OF FEAR *by A.C. Doyle*
MEMORY *by Donald E. Westlake*
NOBODY'S ANGEL *by Jack Clark*
MURDER IS MY BUSINESS *by Brett Halliday*
GETTING OFF *by Lawrence Block*

The
CONSUMMATA

by **Mickey Spillane**
and **Max Allan Collins**

A HARD CASE CRIME NOVEL

A HARD CASE CRIME BOOK
(HCC-103)
First Hard Case Crime edition: October 2011

Published by

Titan Books
A division of Titan Publishing Group Ltd
144 Southwark Street
London SE1 0UP

in collaboration with Winterfall LLC

Print edition ISBN 978-0-85768-288-8
E-book ISBN 978-0-85768-598-8

Design direction by Max Phillips
www.maxphillips.net

Typeset by Swordsmith Productions

The name "Hard Case Crime" and the Hard Case Crime logo
are trademarks of Winterfall LLC. Hard Case Crime books
are selected and edited by Charles Ardai.

Printed in the United States of America

Visit us on the web at www.HardCaseCrime.com

For Lynn Myers —
one of Mickey's
favorite customers

CO-AUTHOR'S NOTE

In 1967, with some fanfare, Mickey Spillane's The Delta Factor*—introducing Morgan the Raider as a new series character—enjoyed considerable critical and commercial success. After a disappointing experience producing a* Factor *film, however, the frustrated Spillane set aside the already-announced second Morgan novel,* The Consummata. *Twenty years ago, he entrusted the incomplete manuscript to me, saying, "Maybe someday we can do something with this."*

Thanks to Charles Ardai of Hard Case Crime, that day is here.

The story is set in the late '60s, when Mickey began it.

THE CONSUMMATA

CHAPTER ONE

They were closing in.

There were two up ahead, another pair behind me, and when I reached the corner the trap would snap shut...and only open again inside a maximum security prison where every contrivance devised by experts knowledgeable in the science of incarceration would be utilized to keep me there the rest of my life.

At least I had given them a run for the taxpayers' money. Still, it was a damn shame this melodrama had to wind up on a side street in Miami with the federal boys having all the advantage, and me with the job I had to do so far from over.

In the reflection of an angled window, I saw a black sedan round the corner behind me and cruise at a walking pace. Modern technology was raising hell with being a fugitive—each two-man team carried an attaché case packed with a communications rig. That kept the pairs fore and aft in touch with the rolling forces as well as other teams that would be blocking off any remaining escape avenues.

It was my own damn fault, but part of the odds I had to face. When you come out into the open, knowing your photo is in every post office, representing a forty-million dollar haul every hood would like to hijack—and that any stool pigeon would like to cash in for big-league brownie points— well, you are *really* bucking the odds.

I had one thing going for me, anyway—this was a capture operation, not a hit. They'd have orders to go all out bringing me back alive, even risking taking on fire themselves. Your life carries a high premium when they think you're the only guy who knows where a forty-mil payday got buried.

Just the same, they had minimized any chance of defeat. Federal suits hit the streets with local fuzz playing back-up—a power play from the second they'd made me.

When exactly they got me in their sights, I didn't know— sometime during the last four days—but now all I could do was lead them down a blind alley as far away as possible from those who had covered for me.

My trackers kept their suitcoats unbuttoned to make for easy access under government threads designed to disguise the artillery beneath their arms. But they weren't as smart as they thought they were. Suits in stifling weather like this? And dark colors, not even going pastel for the season and the locale. Picking out these feds in a Florida crowd was like spotting a turd in a punch bowl.

But all their man- and firepower was unnecessary because I wasn't even packing a rod. They sure were going all out to get their forty million bucks back.

Forty million I never had in the first place.

Overhead, the summer sun had started to snuggle down into its pocket in the west, leaving the heat of day shimmering off the buildings of a neighborhood where white guys in suits didn't belong in the first place. Little cream-in-the-coffee Cuban kids ran around like mice, shrieking and yelling in two languages, bare feet slapping the hot pavement.

The little ones were lucky. One way or another, they had made it off Castro's island with their families and they had freedom now. They were even free to run on the damn sidewalks.

Another half-block and I wouldn't be free at all.

Behind me, the pair closed the gap and the car had picked up the pace. With their blank pale faces and black sunglasses, they were like robots on a programmed course of action. And they were timing it very nicely. There was a surety about their movements that reflected absolute confidence in their maneuver.

Until I had walked them into Little Havana, they probably figured I hadn't smelled them out, and that when they took me, the surprise would be complete. Only now they had to know that *I* knew, and that was not a good thing.

In fact, it put me in a worse place. But when they took me down—and they *would* take me down, all right—I'd at least have the fun of sitting in an interrogation room chair and letting them know how fast I'd got on to them.

"Glad to help you boys out," I'd say. *"Maybe you can be more on the ball next time. Might want to skip the Brooks Brothers in tropical climes."*

And I would have the small pleasure of making them squirm, while they would have the big pleasure of slamming my ass in solitary confinement.

If I had wanted to throw Penny and Lee to the wolves, I could've broken loose; but you don't do that to friends. I had to put distance between myself and those who'd risked everything to shelter me, and play it out with the odds against me, and if I lost, I lost.

It was as simple as that.

Up ahead a pack of little *muchachos* let out a howl of bird squeals as they came tumbling around the side of a building, racing toward me with another pack in pursuit, playing one of their crazy kid games. I paused while they flowed around me, then edged myself toward the wall so the second bunch of brats wouldn't have to use me for an obstacle course.

But suddenly I had become part of their game.

They had me surrounded, with half of the pack pushing and the other half pulling, and somehow under the yelling I could make out a tiny voice whispering, "Go in, *señor*…go inside, *rapidamente!*"

I had time for one quick look around and spotted the first bunch of kids piled up in front of the pair of tails who were trying to pick and claw their way through the mini-mob hanging onto their legs and arms when an adult hand grabbed my shoulder, hauled me through the doorway beside a grocery store, and shoved me into the gloom of a corridor.

The sun outside had been so blinding that the transition threw me into total darkness for a second, but I followed the hand that tugged at my coat, stumbled twice, recovered, then felt myself being guided into a recession in a wall. To call it a closet would be generous.

The voice said, "Stay there. Be quiet, *señor*."

Then something was slammed in place—not a door, more

like a panel—and I had just enough room to feel like I was in an upright coffin.

Out there somewhere, a woman was screaming in anger, her lung power fantastic. She was the lead instrument in a raucous symphony that included babies bawling, kids yelling, feet pounding, furious voices barking orders in English, and only getting in return a chorus of excited Spanish.

A husky male voice said, "Damnit, you people—*shut up*! *You*, lady…cut that yelling, *now!* Jesus Christ. Lou, will you tell them to speak *English*, goddamnit!"

A younger, higher-pitched voice rattled out commands in fluent Spanish and answers came from a dozen mouths. The screaming woman took over after a few seconds, demanding in her shrill, distinctive fashion to know who these invaders were.

In the momentary lull, I knew the feds must be flashing their fancy credentials.

In Spanish the woman intoned in a mix of sarcasm and resignation, "So—the militia. Your type, they are here only two ways—when they are not needed, or when they are too late. Where were *you*, when that crazy *gringo* came running in here and knocked everybody and everything over? The children, too! Did you see what your madman did to our little ones? Knocking them over like dolls? But, *no*—of course you don't see!"

"Ma'am…."

"No, you stop in the street to play *games* with them. Should we thank you for such attention? You play games, then finally you come pushing in here and make all the noise, and now the *bambinos*, they will *never* get to sleep. The customers, they will stay away today because of the crazy white one running through, knocking over things and people! You militia, you are of such *great* help…"

"Take it easy, *señora*. Take a breath, and tell us what happened."

She took the breath. "He ran out through the back. What do you think? If you had been here, you would see!" She paused, perhaps to point the way. "And that is what happened while you were playing games with our children. Now you stand here and waste even *more* time…"

Somebody swore, then the husky voice again: "Jesus, lady…stand here and listen to your nonsense and we *are* wasting time…Jack, Roger, go out there through the back, where she indicated. Lou, call the locals to close in around the area. I'll take Marty and Pete and shake this place down."

The one called Lou said, "Relax, Bud. Everybody's converging. We're on top of this."

"Are we really? You could fool me."

"Bud, a bat couldn't fly out of here now."

A disgusted grunt. "You must think we're playing with a kid, Lou. Did you read the damn data? This Morgan character's a regular Houdini. How do you think he engineered that *last* escape?"

"This isn't the last escape."

"No, it's a brand-new one." A deep sigh. "Special Agent in Charge Crowley made it clear—he wants Morgan caught, and turned over. He wants some other agency to hold the damn receipt for Morgan's body."

Standing there in total darkness, like a tin soldier in a too-tight toy box, I felt my mouth twist in a grin.

So it was Crowley—the guy who was supposed to have delivered me back into a thirty-year stretch, after I did Uncle Sam that little favor that cut my sentence in half. Or *would* have, if I hadn't escaped instead.

The last time I saw Crowley, he had a wild, surprised look, finding himself stretched out on the cabin floor, a look that got even more surprised as I bailed out over the ocean....

Crowley. I'd have to keep him in mind. At the time, he'd struck me as a guy with the bland face of a professional who would kill if necessary and who you couldn't easily fake out.

A top hand—and he'd *have* to be, if they'd selected him to take delivery on Morgan the Raider. My mission had been a joint venture of the CIA and FBI and assorted other government alphabet soup, and losing a prisoner this important was not going to help out Crowley's career path...

Maybe I'd been wrong about the capture priority. Maybe everything *was* on the line now, and this time Crowley wouldn't worry too much about taking me alive, forty mil or no forty mil. After all, that receipt just specified my body.

Being alive or dead wasn't mentioned.

I could only wonder how long I was going to have to play mummy in this sarcophagus. Hours ago I had gotten cramped from remaining immobile and managed to work myself into a half-squat, knees and back jammed against the sides of the enclosure to relieve my aching muscles.

The passage of time I could only figure from the smells.

Two times the odors of cooking drifted into my tiny compartment, so I must have been stuffed in there for the rest of the day—thank God I'd emptied my bladder before leaving the safe house this morning.

At first the food smells had been a source of annoyance, thick and spicy enough to be an irritant, making me want to sneeze. Now they were tantalizing tempters because my stomach was flat in its emptiness and what at first had seemed distasteful now seemed potentially delicious.

I had lived with thirst before and knew how to control it. Right now, though, I could use a drink, and it wasn't water I wanted, but a tall, cold beer in a frosted glass with the suds running down the sides....

For some reason the cramped quarters weren't as stifling hot as I had expected them to get. The floorboards didn't join and a coolness seemed to seep upward, musty but easy to live with, like being stuck in an old root cellar.

During the first eight hours, dozens of feet had tramped through the premises, adding to the confusion of voices. Somebody was continually chasing the kids out, trying to mollify the protests of the residents. Twice, agents had stood right outside my cubicle and discussed the search, angry voices muffled but very audible.

"These spics snowed us," the husky-voiced one called Bud had said. "They were *in* on it."

"You think these people arranged Morgan's escape?"

That was the one called Lou, and I found myself grinning. Bud and Lou. Abbott and Costello. I began picturing them that way.

"That's what I think," Bud said.

"How the hell did they manage it?"

"The kids were in on it."

"Get serious! The kids? They're too little, too young. They couldn't organize a burping contest."

"Those little bastards did it, Lou, I'm telling you."

"No *way*, Bud—there wasn't time to plan."

"*They* didn't plan it, Lou—the grown-ups did."

"Bud, kids don't react to orders like that! Not in a matter of seconds. Morgan spotted his tail, took advantage of the situation, used those kids for cover, and somehow got through the cordon."

"But *how* did he get through the cordon?"

Who's on first?

A neighborhood house-to-house search was instituted and the feds went through the routine again. Then I heard a voice that echoed back from the recent past and I felt that grin pull at my mouth again.

Crowley.

The big cheese had taken personal charge and everybody was catching hell. As a matter of policy, they were going to station some people around in case I was still holed up, but their own damn self-assurance in their techniques was going to screw the pooch for them.

"It's just precautionary," Crowley said, referring to keeping a minimal presence in the neighborhood. His voice was as bland as my memory of his face. "Morgan's gone. He knew he was being tailed, and walked us into an area where he had allies and resources, and he's far, far gone. You all know his dossier—if we want him back, we have to start from scratch."

So I stayed where I was and listened to the sounds coming back to normal. It would be dark out now, and supper was finished. Faintly, the sounds of a television program came through to me—seemed my saviors watched Johnny Carson, like all good Americans, so I knew it was after eleven o'clock.

I waited.

I changed positions a few times.

And I waited some more.

Then I heard the scratching at the boards in front of my face. I had been in the dark so long my night vision was at its fullest and I saw the section move and slide outward and looked at the funny little guy with the scraggly mustache in the loose light-blue short-sleeve shirt and baggy darker blue pants, standing there trying to peer inside like some fool searching for a missing cat.

He said, "*Señor*…?"

"I'm here." After all those hours, my voice was scratchy.

His bandito mustache rose in a big smile. "Ha, I knew you were not going anywhere, *señor*! But at first I thought you might have lose the conscious, or maybe you were wounded and we did not know, and some terrible thing happen and…"

"*Amigo*, I've never been better. Nothing wounded but my pride."

A relieved sigh.

Then he pulled the boards back farther. "Come out now, quickly, please. It is all right."

I shouldered through the opening, watched while he fitted what appeared to be part of the wall back in place. Then he shoved a carton of garbage up against it and I followed him through a grocery storeroom and up a dark flight of stairs, and into more darkness.

After he bolted the door behind us, he flicked on a yellow-shaded lamp beside an ancient radio console. The room was small but not tiny, with adobe-type walls, second-hand furniture and Catholic wall decorations.

Then my host turned to study me, his face bright with pleasure.

His half-bow was almost comic. "Allow me to present myself, *señor*. I am Pedro Navarro, formerly of Cuba, but now a citizen of your country by choice."

"I'm Morgan," I said.

That smile blossomed under the mustache again—somewhat yellow, like the lamp shade. He was a smoker—the smell of cigars was on him. Well, he *was* Cuban....

We sat on a couch whose springs were too tired to complain, and cold beers were drawn from a cooler, ice cold, sweaty in a good way, and he let me swallow one down before he got me another. I was just nursing that one when he picked up the conversation.

"*Señor* Morgan, of course I know who you are. The man with but one name. Morgan the Raider, the militia keep calling you. A pirate for our day. But we do not reveal what we know of you in front of the intruders. We think that is more wise."

Being known at all was something I wanted no part of. Why did a bunch of Cuban exiles know who the hell I was? There were too many possibilities, none of them good.

I said, "Why should you know me, Pedro? I've kind of

made a point of staying under the radar. Only cops and crooks know who I am…or anyway, that's what I thought."

"It is more a matter of knowing *of* you, *Señor* Morgan. Until now, none of us have had the pleasure of meeting you. But we are glad to do so now."

"Why?"

He caught the look in my eyes and smiled again. "Some months ago you did our neighboring country, Nuevo Cadiz, a great service. There you have become a legend. They sing of you in the cantinas, they write your name on the wall."

"Not restroom walls, I hope."

He didn't get the joke and seemed momentarily dismayed. "No, no, you are a *hero* in that country!"

I had to smirk. "Probably not to everybody."

"This is true, *Señor* Morgan. To certain people connected with the former corrupt government, to mention your name to them is to make them ill in the stomach, no? They talk of you in Cuba, too, where the people hope and dream that perhaps one day you might honor them with your presence, your talents, and give those thieves in control…" He paused and spat on the floor with vehemence. "…the taste of *death* they deserve."

"I have no business in Cuba, *amigo*."

His head nodded in sad agreement. "A man's business is his own. His choices are his to make. We all know this."

"Good."

"But, *señor*, to Cubans, you are still a symbol. Someone to be admired, even to be…imitated. A great hero makes small heroes out of others, and enough small heroes can be…"

"An army of revolution?"

"Yes. And those heroes, they will arise when the time comes."

I tried to make sure my smile didn't seem patronizing. I owed this guy, and his people.

"Friend," I said, "you're talking to a man with a price on his head and the police at his back. I'm about as helpful to you right now as a rabid dog. If the *federales* knew what you did for me? Hell, they'd slap you in the pen so fast your eyes would cross."

His smile blossomed again, but melancholy now. "Ah, again true. But the people who helped you, who look up to you, they do not care. They brush up against a real hero, and they help this hero, and they feel good about themselves and each other."

"Yeah, well, whatever works for them." I swallowed more beer. "How did *you* work it, Pedro?"

Navarro's shrug was a masterpiece of understatement. "Heroes are recognized…by police and populace alike. There was one of our people…he was in Nuevo Cadiz, when you staged your small revolution, *señor*, and when he saw you on the street here he recognized you…knew you at once."

"A break for me."

"And he saw those who followed you, too, and when you headed our way, we were called…and called to *action*. In just a few minutes, several things were planned for coming to your assistance."

I let out a little laugh. They sure had done a great job on the fly like that.

"You see, we are good Americans, *Señor* Morgan, but we know that police, those with badges, don't always work for... what is the phrase? The public interest. And American or not, we are still Cubans. And the hero of Nuevo Cadiz, well ...we have more loyalty to him than to *any* militia."

I had to laugh again. "My God, were those kids really in on it from the start?"

"Ah, yes, the children. The police didn't believe the little ones could be organized like that. They forgot one thing. These *muchachos* grew up in the knowledge of much injustice. Only because of lessons learned in the streets of Havana are these children here in America with the rest of us."

Well, Sherlock Holmes had his Baker Street Irregulars. Now Morgan the Raider had his own little Cuban pirates to thank.

I shook my head. "How in the hell do I find a way to say *gracias*, Pedro? For what you and your people have done?"

That shrug again. "There is no need. You may thank us by not being caught, and by remaining an inspiration to a beaten-down people and perhaps to keep in your mind that there are such people, and that they need you.

"They can look up to me if they like. There's no accounting for taste. But there isn't much chance of me helping anybody out. A guy in a hole has enough trouble digging himself out."

"But, *señor*, people in the premature grave, they...what is the expression? Perhaps they should stick together. It is a thought, no?"

Now it was my turn to shrug. "If it pleases you."

He stared at me a long moment, then said, "Tell me, *Señor* Morgan, is it true you stole forty million dollars from your government, and have it hidden in some safe place?"

I chuckled. "That would buy a nice little invasion army, wouldn't it, Pedro?"

He laughed, too, shook his head, and finally sipped his own beer. "A *very* nice army, possibly even a successful one...but we are content to raise our own funds through our own efforts."

"If you're not asking for a handout, from that forty mil, why do you bring it up?"

"I am a curious man, *senor*."

Apparently he hadn't heard about the cat.

"Sorry, Pedro, I hate to disappoint you. It's true the... militia...thinks I pulled that job. But I never did. Hope it doesn't spoil my image, buddy."

His teeth gleamed brightly under his mustache. "I wouldn't have believed you, *senor*, if you told me that you *did* do this thing."

"Why not?"

"*Señor*...surely you know the stories about you, they say you are the robbing hood."

I almost choked on my beer. "Yeah. I'm a robbin' hood, all right. I never took any spoils from anybody who didn't have it coming. Criminals, bad people in general with money and jewels and other goodies that they didn't earn or deserve...I took it from them."

"And gave to the poor, *senor*?"

"Well...sort of. At first, *I* was poor, remember. But no,

Pedro, I'm no saint. I'm the raider they say I am. I just don't knock over solid citizens, much less Uncle Whiskers."

"Uncle…?"

"Uncle Sugar. Uncle Sam?"

"Ah!" He pointed at me. "He wants you!"

"Doesn't he, though."

He stood. "We will serve you a meal now, *señor*, if you will so honor us."

"That growling you hear is my stomach thanking you in advance."

I got up and stuck my hand out and he shook it. Stood there just looking down at this little guy who was, as far as I was concerned, seven feet tall.

"After we eat, *Señor* Morgan, we must prepare you for your departure. The militia are still about, so you will remain here until we are sure it is safe for you to leave."

"You're sticking your neck out pretty far."

"That is not a new experience, *señor*," he said with his smile turned sideways. "Your accommodations will not be lavish, I am sorry to say — simply a secret space off the bedroom of my wife and me…but quite safe. They have already searched there twice and have not found it. And it will be more spacious than your other hiding place."

That wouldn't be tough.

"Mind answering me something, Pedro?"

"Most certainly."

"Why the necessity for all these hiding places?"

For a moment he said nothing—he had his own secrets.

But then he shrugged again. "We, too, are fighting an

enemy. We are not pursued, and yet, in our way, we are fugitives."

I nodded. "Chased from your homes."

"Our homeland has been ravaged, our properties confiscated, friends and relatives executed. Even in this country, the enemy has ways of getting to those it considers a threat. At such times, *señor*, a hiding place is most necessary. The place where you were housed before? That was previously used to keep our limited treasury."

My eyebrows went up. "Your treasury's pretty damn empty, if you can fit me in there."

Now the smile disappeared. His face grew tight, his eyes black with hatred. "Once it was…what is the word? Flush. A small treasure a pirate such as yourself might find well worth…raiding. Treasure that would have bought the safety of many lives."

"What happened to it?"

"Money that can be the source of much good is often a lure for evil. It was stolen, *señor*."

"Who did it?"

"His name is Jaimie Halaquez. A bad man, *señor*. A devil that walks the earth. A man I would kill with these hands, if I had the chance, with no fear of losing my place in Heaven."

He held his hands before him and strangled the air.

Then his grip loosened into fingers and the bitterness that etched his face disappeared and he smiled again.

"Come, *Señor* Morgan—you must eat. It has been a long time for you, between meals, no? But there was no other way. You need to seem to be gone. Vanished. And we need to appear as simple, unknowing peasants, not harborers of fugitives. And I do apologize for you having to stay for so long in that...that coffin."

"It's okay, Pedro."

"It is?"

"Yeah. Any coffin you can crawl back out of? That's one of your better coffins."

This joke he got, and he led me into the next room, where a small feast awaited. I may not have been the hero they made me out to be, but I wasn't about to turn down this delicious a hero's welcome.

CHAPTER TWO

The federal prosecutors had not been shy about discussing the criminal-style activities I'd conducted for my country during the war. That was the heart of their case against me, after all. The shipment of currency from the Washington mint to New York consisted of forty million dollars in common bills, a paper volume that filled a medium-sized armored truck.

Why the G had made me for the heist was simple—I had pulled similar scores twice, during the war, getting troop-movement plans and coordinates on German blockhouses from their armored cars—utilizing booby-trap gimmicks to stop vehicles at given points, D-Y gas to knock out the drivers and passengers, with the means of entry a compact torch unit the Allied command had executed for me from my schematics. Complicated heists, requiring six-man teams.

Those two hits provided the template for the money truck score, right down to the torch.

So all these years later, a grateful government sent me to maximum security…only they hadn't been able to keep me there; and the next time the "militia" had caught up with me had been dumb luck on their part, and rotten luck on mine.

They'd tried to do it through know-how and technology—first the NYPD, because the Big Apple was where the hijacking went down, then every great government agency you ever heard of and several you haven't, and all the resources that implies.

And they hadn't been alone—private investigators lured by the reward got in the fray, and Mob types who figured they could slam me in a chair, give me a blow-torch refresher, and get the location of the hidden loot out of me.

Nobody had succeeded.

Luck had prevailed where skill had failed. Luck in the form of a coked-up kid in a stolen heap in a high-speed chase with a squad car that spooked the driver into making too wide and wild a turn, sending himself over the curb and the heap onto its skidding side, taking one not-so-innocent bystander along for the ride through a store window in a shower of glass.

Luck.

You can't buy it. And you can't avoid it. It finds you, and does its capricious thing, a coin flip coming up tails and giving you the bad luck of getting clipped by that coke freak, only to come up heads and let you survive, with just a minor concussion, cuts, abrasions, and a couple broken ribs. No internal injuries at all.

Luck.

The coin flips again, comes up tails, and an intern looking for a gold star goes to the trouble of fingerprinting an accident victim whose I.D. somehow got lost in the shuffle, and those prints get sent to a local precinct house and on to Washington, and you? You're not even awake yet.

And when you do wake up, that coin has come up tails

again, and you're back in the less than loving arms of your Uncle Sam.

So I'd agreed to take on the Nuevo Cadiz mission. The end game was getting a top research scientist out of a supposedly impenetrable prison called the Rose Castle. My ability to break out of prisons suggested to the federal boys that I might be able to just as effectively break into one.

The deal was I'd get fifteen years off my thirty-year sentence. And as deals went, it stunk. But I liked the idea of the government paying for a Caribbean vacation, and I also liked the odds of me slipping their grip at the end of the mission....

Nuevo Cadiz was Cuba before the revolution, a dictatorship flush with the dough brought in by casino-driven tourist trade. A good number of those tourists were hoodlums on the run, paying for the privilege of sanctuary, and mobsters using the casinos as money laundries. I went in as one of those shady tourists, a guy who maybe had forty mil to fence. My CIA handlers teamed me with one Kimberly Stacy, an agent who would travel along as my wife. To keep the cover authentic, Kim Stacy and I got married in Georgia by a justice of the peace.

We were still married, Kim and me.

My lovely doll of a bride would never have made it in the fashion mags—not tall enough, and way too many curves... long dark sun-streaked hair tumbling to her shoulders, her face an oval blessed with large almond eyes, as violet as Liz Taylor's, a small, well-carved nose, and a lush mouth that could convey wry amusement with just the slightest rise at either corner.

I could close my eyes and see her in our Nuevo Cadiz hotel room, staring up at me from the bed, lounging in that sheer black negligee, its nylon hugging her with static insistence, a bottle of champagne nearby, the radio whispering Latin rhythms.

But all for show. To make the honeymoon look good.

On an early meeting, in the planning stages, I'd asked her casually if there were any "special instructions" on this assignment.

"What do you mean?" Her voice throaty, sultry.

"I mean, are we going to consummate this marriage?"

The burn started at her sweet throat and rose to her cheeks. "When I have a man, it's at my choosing."

I'd told her that was smart.

Smart? she'd asked.

Yeah, I said, *the Company knows non-consummation makes perfect grounds for annulment or divorce. But they forgot one thing.*

Oh?

Yeah, I said, grinning, *it's damn hard to charge a husband for raping his wife.*

That was when she showed me the little gun.

And I remembered what one of the feds had told me about her: that Kim Stacy had shot and killed five men on previous assignments, that she was trained in all the martial arts and weaponry, and that her skills got her rated as one of the company's best operatives.

But as the mission progressed, she warmed to me, and my warped sense of humor. By the time I was putting that scientist on that little plane on a runway whipped with gusts announcing a coming hurricane, Kim loved me. And I loved her.

We'd gone through hell together, in just a few days, but the heaven of consummating that love, and our marriage, hadn't happened. Just the same, we were man and wife now.

Before I jumped into the sky over the ocean, I told her. Told her that even though she now knew I hadn't pulled that heist, I would never be able to clear myself with her bosses till I recovered that missing forty mil.

"You'll have to wait for me," I told her.

"Forever if I have to," she'd said.

But now I could only wonder...*would I ever see my wife again?*

Pedro's wife Maria was the one with the powerful lungs whose screaming complaints had made the militia's life so miserable, not long ago.

Sitting across from her, my belly bursting with black beans, rice and Ropa Viela—beef that to me looked like Carolina pulled pork—I could make out the voluptuous beauty she'd once been, before her own good cooking got away from her.

She was still a handsome woman, towering over her husband, with liquid brown eyes buried in happy folds of fat that gave her face the appearance of a big baby's. When she was sure the two men at her table had both had their fill, she was content to sit back and watch us placidly smoke Cuban cigars and drink cold beer. Now and again, she would nod as

Pedro recounted their years together, before Castro.

They had been prosperous farmers then, but the loss of their station hadn't put a schism in their relationship. Today Pedro owned the grocery store below us as well as operating a successful garage, using knowledge acquired fixing tractors on his farm, and Maria seemed more proud of him than ever. If these two were a sample of the Cuban refugee situation, then there was no problem in our side accepting Castro's rejects.

Somehow Pedro managed to turn the conversation around to me. No details about the Rose Castle escape had ever seen publication, but his intimate knowledge of pertinent facts meant he had a real pipeline into Nuevo Cadiz. When Maria saw me squirm under her husband's compliments, she silenced him with a wave of her pudgy hand.

Her rosebud mouth pursed into a smile. "They tell us, *señor*, of a woman, a very beautiful woman who was at your side in Nuevo Cadiz. She was your wife, they say."

Even just the mention of her was jolting. Kim, with the wild, glossy black hair, the outrageously perfect body, eyes that could mix all the emotions at once and unleash them through the moist warmth of those full lips.

"She was my wife," I said quietly.

Maria's eyes studied my face and what she saw there brought the faintest frown to her forehead. "*Truly* your wife?"

Pedro winced.

"We were married," I said. "It was part of…do you understand what I mean by cover story?"

"*Si,*" she said as she nodded. "Still…you loved her, no?"

"I loved her, yes."

Pedro sat forward. "Maria…"

She cut her husband off with another wave. "And she…?"

"She loved me, all right."

"But was your union…how do you say, *matrimonio consumado*?"

"We never got the chance," I said with a sad smile.

A flush of indignation spread across Pedro's face and he half-rose from his chair. "Maria! There are matters one prefers not to discuss in polite company. These things, they are most personal, and—"

"Oh, be still, Pedro, my little donkey. There are matters of which men know nothing at all. They must be led like children. They must be—"

"Maria!"

"It's okay, Pedro," I said, not offended. I looked across at Maria and let the ache in my chest die down. "Like I say, I was forced to marry her—so the job could be done. It had to…look *real*."

"But you said you loved each other," she reminded me.

"Things were…different then. We were caught up in something bigger than we were. It was exciting and dangerous. That kind of thing plays hell with your thinking. If she's smart, she'll have forgotten all about me."

The voluptuous beauty she'd once been peered out from inside the fat woman, and eyes that knew lust and love met mine. "I do not think, *Señor* Morgan, that any woman, she can forget you."

Pedro, frowning, sighed, and made a gesture of apology to me.

I ignored him, and told her, "Maybe she'll be lucky, then."

"Losing a man such as you, *señor*, would not be lucky."

"Kim was a decent woman, courageous and on the right side of the fence. Face it, *amigos*, I'm a first-class hood. I've done time, and if I get nailed, I'll do plenty more. You think I want her to have any part of me?"

Maria shook her head sadly. "That question is for *her* to answer."

"She won't get the chance, *mamacita*. I love her enough to want her out of my life. For her own good."

There was something else my hostess wanted to say, but somewhere a buzzer hummed two short bursts, and Maria stopped her question abruptly.

Pedro's head snapped around, he glanced at his wife, then pushed his chair back. He saw the way I was sitting there, tense, hands gripping the edge of the table, and he squeezed my shoulder.

"This is nothing concerning you, *Señor* Morgan. It is another matter entirely. Stay there, *por favor*."

He got up, walked into the next room, and I heard a door open and shut quietly.

With a calming gesture, Maria said, "The buzzer that you hear? It is one used only by our friends."

Within a minute Pedro was back again. He came into the room first, made sure nothing had changed, then stepped aside and nodded.

The man with him could have been anywhere from forty

to sixty. He was taller than Pedro, his carriage erect, his gaze sharp, a slender dignified figure in a dark suit and white shirt with a bolo tie. He let his eyes take in every detail of the room before he seemed to relax.

Time or something else had shot his hair with strands of white and some of the lines that etched his face hadn't been put there by the years. His trim mustache with spade beard, however, was black as a raven's wing. There was something familiar about him that I couldn't place.

And one thing I didn't want to see right now was a familiar face. If I knew someone, then he had to know me.

I didn't have to say a word. He seemed to read my mind and smiled gently. "It seems we are two of a kind, *señor.* We recognize what lies below the surface. May I introduce myself? I am Luis Saladar, late of the Republic of Cuba."

Then I remembered him. We had never met, but I *did* remember him....

He had fought both Batista and Castro, though the guns against his opposition party were too big and too many. His supporters had broken him out of one of Castro's jails the day before he was to be executed. He had asked for political asylum in this country and gotten it.

Only now the feds were looking for Saladar under a deportation order, because he had been trying to organize another revolutionary group to invade Cuba and the doves in government were too jittery to upset the status quo. After the Bay of Pigs, the Missile Crisis, and the Kennedy assassination, our government's Cuban operations had been curtailed. The current White House would rather let the menace exist ninety miles off our coastline than risk any more problems with Russia.

"Morgan," I said and held out my hand. "I guess we *are* two of a kind."

His grip was firm, his eyes steady on mine. "I realize your situation here, *señor*. Let me assure you that I took every precaution not to be observed. There are still police about, but I was not seen."

"You sound sure of yourself."

He smiled wryly. "I have an advantage. Cubans in a Cuban community all seem to look alike to certain of your countrymen."

"Well, I can tell the difference," I said, grinning back at him, "but I'm not an idiot."

He chuckled, then sat down next to Pedro.

"Hey, if you have business to discuss," I said, half-rising, "I can crawl back in my hidey-hole."

"No, please," Saladar told me with an upraised palm and embarrassed expression. "I, too, have occupied those cramped quarters. There is no reason for you to be uncomfortable any longer than necessary. Besides, *señor*, it is possible you might be in a position to advise us…if you would be so kind. Your presence here comes at a most fortunate moment."

"*Amigo*," I said, shaking my head, "I'm far from an expert on the political situation."

"Politics are not the issue, *señor*." Saladar's expression turned grave. "It is a matter of thievery."

I nodded. "Your old '*amigo*' Jaimie Halaquez?"

Pedro and Luis exchanged glances.

Saladar said, "You are quite astute, *señor*."

"Pedro mentioned him earlier. How much did the bastard get?"

Saladar sighed. "Seventy-five thousand dollars."

I raised one eyebrow. It wasn't enough dough to raise them both.

"That's not a fortune," I said. "But it's a lot to be collected in an impoverished area like this."

Saladar folded his hands on his flat belly and leaned back. There was sadness in his eyes.

"*Señor* Morgan, you are correct. That figure represents very many pennies and nickels, carefully saved from meager earnings. It represents hours of extra work for the privilege of contributing to the fund. For many, it means that clothes must be mended some more, and the table spread with a little less. Yet it was money cheerfully given so that others could escape the oppression they now face." He shook his head. "This was more than simple thievery, *señor*. It was a tragedy."

"Sorry, *amigo*." I didn't let him off the hook. "You shouldn't have picked such a lousy, lowlife character to handle your cash."

"In hindsight, this is obvious. But at the time...who was to know?"

I shook my head at him, still not letting him off. "You've been to the rodeo plenty of times, Luis. Okay if I call you 'Luis'? I mean no disrespect."

He lowered his head, held up his hand, granting permission.

"It's not like you haven't had experience in such things," I said. "I mean, I figure you must have known this Halaquez guy pretty well. And nobody made him for a stinker?"

Saladar's smile had a grim twist to it. "We *thought* we knew him well, and we detected no…unfortunate fragrance." The knuckles of his fingers were white.

"*Señor* Morgan," Pedro said, sitting forward, "Jaimie Halaquez…our '*amigo*' as you call him…was working for the present Cuban government. It was Jaimie's job to keep his masters informed of our movements. But…he came here and he *told* us of this."

"A double agent," I said.

Pedro nodded. "He would inform us of their plans—the Castro people *do* carry out activities in Miami, *señor*, in particular trying to…what is the word? Infiltrate our ranks."

"Not surprising," I said.

"Ever since the takeover," Pedro continued, "he has been one of us. It was through Halaquez that we were able to make contact with our families and sympathizers, back home…because he had access to Cuba. Until now, the information he brought to us appeared true, and whatever he gave to his Cuban masters about us was either false or distorted. His work on our behalf, it was always done well."

"Until now," I said.

Something desperate came into Pedro's tone as he gestured with two open palms. "We thought him trustworthy."

I slowly scanned their faces, then nodded. "You've been gathering money for a long time, taking precautions. Everybody in your circle knew about it, and since you admit you may have infiltrators, you were careful."

Pedro sighed. "But not careful enough. It is difficult when one you trust betrays you."

I'd been there. "You've had your treasury heisted before, haven't you?"

"Unfortunately, yes."

"By these infiltrators you mentioned?"

"In one case, yes. In the two other instances, they were simply greedy fools. This is the fourth…what is the word… setback? Setback in as many years."

"What happened to the others who stole from you, Pedro?"

"They were caught by our people. Their captors had a hot-blooded temperament, *señor*, and while one despairs of such things…the traitors' deaths were justified."

"And the money they stole?"

"Always there was enough time for them to spend it or…"

Pedro searched for the word.

"Transfer," Saladar offered.

"Transfer it," Pedro said, with a nod of thanks to his friend. "However, the amounts that were stolen before— and the need for funds—were as *nothing* compared to this."

I shook my head in disgust. "You've been raided, my friends. It's an old operation."

All three looked at me, puzzled.

"Your *amigo* Halaquez played the game. He knew he had suckers on the line, so he just wormed his way in and waited you out. You collected the money, he took delivery, and he'll get it through to Cuba, all right. The only difference is, the loot won't go to your friends and families there who need the help."

They all frowned, but it was Saladar who said, "What do you mean, *señor*?"

"I mean, it'll buy Jaimie some favor with the Castro crowd, and maybe put him up in high society. Hell, when you're in favor and eating high off the hog, Havana isn't a bad place to live, even now. He can already come and go as he pleases, only this time when he goes back, he won't return. Why should he? He'll stay there and live it up. Come back to the States, he gets bumped off."

For a few moments nobody spoke.

Finally Saladar said, "Perhaps you have a suggestion, *Señor* Morgan."

"Sure," I said. "Start up another collection."

The futility of it brought a bitter laugh to Saladar's mouth. "Another year of sacrifice for our people? It will be bad enough when they learn of this, this…treachery. After yet another failure, who will trust us to act on their behalf?"

I frowned. "You haven't told your people here that their contributions were snatched?"

Saladar shook his head firmly, frowning. "Do you realize how many here are making preparations to see their families again? Others long to help relieve the miseries at home, and see their people fed, and for medicines to be made available…to give hope that one day Cuba will be liberated from the madmen who rule over them."

"Sooner or later they're going to get wise."

Saladar nodded solemnly. "We have until that day to look for Jaimie Halaquez."

I felt that funny little touch of excitement again. It was like sensing a ship over the horizon. You couldn't see it, but you knew it was there. The anticipation of a raid. Then I felt pretty damned ashamed of myself, and wiped the feeling away.

I said, "You can't mean the son of a bitch is still *around*? With that much swag on hand?"

"We frankly do not know, *señor*," Saladar said softly. "We *do* know Halaquez has not reached Cuba yet. Where he is, in *this* country? We have no notion…but our sources on the island tell us he most certainly is *not* there."

"Maybe I had it wrong," I admitted. "Maybe he isn't going to live the Havana high life. Easy enough for him to spend that money in the States, *amigos*, even if it wouldn't go as far."

But Saladar was shaking his head. "Unlikely, *Señor* Morgan. Our people are diversified now. They have taken jobs in every state in the union. Key people have been alerted, and if Halaquez tries to spend our money here in the States? Well, then, we will have him."

"Is that likely?"

"Unfortunately, no—he is smarter than that—it is like you say before, *señor*…to get the most out of that money, he must return to Cuba. As for now, he is…hiding out. Lying low." He paused a second and watched me carefully. "That is why I ask if you have a suggestion."

"For locating Halaquez?"

"Exactly."

I grinned at him. "Tell me something, Luis. Did you guys use ESP or something, to lead me here?"

Saladar didn't see the humor. "No, my friend. We are simply taking advantage of an opportunity. Naturally, I learned at once of your presence here. I am fully aware of your past history. That is why I ask you for the suggestion. In these matters, you are the expert, the professional."

"Not in the political arena, *amigo*. Sorry to disappoint."

Once again Saladar paused and leaned forward, his hands still clenched. "Know this, *Señor* Morgan, we do not seek repayment for aiding you. You need to banish any such thought from your mind."

"Okay."

"We will make sure you escape from this place. We do so with gratitude. We are your true friends."

"You've proved it, Luis."

He smiled and it was a sly thing. "So…can not a friend ask another friend for a suggestion? Whatever you say, we will attempt to do. At this point, we are desperate for a solution."

"I won't suggest anything," I said.

His eyes grew a little sad. "Very well. May I ask why?"

I held up a hand. "Because somebody might get hurt taking my advice. Like you said, I'm the pro. A generous definition for a hood, but apt enough."

"We can try our best."

"No."

He started to cover his disappointment with a shrug, then I added, "I'll do it myself."

His eyes widened abruptly and he unlocked his fingers and ran them through his hair. "No, *señor*, it will be enough for you merely to escape. You cannot jeopardize yourself on our account."

I laughed, once. "Hell, it'll keep me in practice."

"Your suggestion would be enough, *señor*. Tell us what to do and—"

"My suggestion is you listen to the pro. You can conduct your own search in your own way, and if you're smart, you'll get one of the friendlier police agencies to help you. You want to go that route, fine."

"We do not."

"Then I have my own methods and my own contacts and I don't want any amateurs screwing them up."

"*Señor...*"

I cocked my head. "That is, unless you're afraid to let me loose on this thing."

They glanced at each other, then back to me. "Why would that be, *señor*?"

"Maybe if I get my hands on that dough, I'll just take off with it myself."

Because I was grinning at them, they didn't take it as an offense. Both of them smiled back and Maria's smile was the biggest of all.

Finally Saladar said, "No, *señor*, we are not afraid of that at all. You are a man of honor."

I was glad I wasn't taking a swig of beer when he said that. "Say that in front of *some* people," I said, "and you'll get the biggest laugh of your life."

There was silence for a moment, then Saladar reached in his inside suitcoat pocket and withdrew an envelope. He opened it on the table and bills spilled out.

"Jaimie Halaquez did not find everything, *Señor* Morgan," he said. "To do what you must do, you will need money. Here is the last of it—five thousand dollars. I trust it will be enough to serve the purpose."

"You're a trusting group."

Saladar nodded. "That is our nature, *señor*. Our mistake before was not picking the *right* one to trust."

"You could be making the same mistake now."

"We don't think so."

"I tell you what." I reached for the bills and tucked them back into the envelope. "We'll call this a down payment. Toward fifteen percent of what I recover."

"That is fair, *señor*," Saladar said.

"If I don't get your money back," I said, "I reimburse you for everything but expenses. Okay?"

"You are too generous," Pedro said.

"Not really. Got a picture of this character?"

They did. A snapshot taken a street festival right here in Little Havana—Jaimie Halaquez had an arm around Pedro and they were all smiles. Wearing a black leather vest over a purple shirt, his hair a long, perfect, shining black crown, Halaquez stood a head higher than Pedro, loomed above everyone around him. A handsome son of a bitch, but for a boxer's pushed-in nose and a jagged scar on one cheek.

"Can you find him, *señor*?" Maria asked, wearing the same expression she no doubt wore to mass. "Can you return what he took from us?"

"Well, I can't get back the betrayed loyalty. But the money I have a shot at." I slipped the photo in a pocket, then gestured with the envelope of bills. "And tell you what—if I have to kill your *amigo* Jaimie Halaquez, along the way?"

Saladar said, "Yes, *señor*?"

"Well, I'll just toss that in."

And I pocketed the five thou.

CHAPTER THREE

Getting through the loosened cordon that still peppered the area wouldn't be too hard—not when you had the back alley knowledge my escort did.

In the dim, soft light of the back room of the building where Pedro and Maria lived, I had been delivered to this lovely little chaperone with no ceremony, just quick, explicit instructions. The small dark-haired wench had a lithe, cuddly look, but when you touched her, there was no softness there at all.

She could have passed for one of those sudden-blooming Latin women who are mature at fifteen, at least until the light caught her face just right and illuminated her expression as she passed judgment on me, bringing her years into view.

She was thirty, easy.

Her eyes were black and challenging, framed under rounded V's of brows that seemed like birds in startled flight. There was a natural high rise to her cheekbones and a mouth barren of lipstick, yet lush and blushed with a sensual red, courtesy of God, not Max Factor.

The clothes she wore were loose-fitting with a gypsy swirl to them, pastel greens and browns, though she was born to wear red. And those loose threads couldn't hide the pert tilt of full breasts nor the tight, nipped-in waist that flared into miniature Madonna hips.

They called her Gaita, but I knew that wasn't her name—kitten, it meant. But this was a sex kitten grown into full-scale cat, with the claws and purring intact—I hoped she had most of her nine lives left, for what lay ahead.

I was in greasy coveralls that had *Farango Car Wash* stitched across the back. I wore makeup and a spirit-gummed-on gaucho mustache that wouldn't work on Broadway but should do just fine in dark byways.

I had said to Pedro, "It's not the local police I'm worried about. They've got no stake in this. By now, they'll be pulled back to their normal duties."

Pedro nodded. "It has been explained, my friend. This one, Gaita, knows where the local militia are posted. And we have spotted the outsiders who hunt you as well."

"Good."

"If necessary, others will help, too. Remember, we are all too familiar with authority's *perros de caza*. They are true hunters. At nothing will they stop." His brief smile was reassuring. "Nor will we."

Under my breath I said, "This girl, she knows the drill? And understands the danger?"

"Oh yes. You may trust Gaita."

But now, barely half an hour later, I was wondering just how far I could trust her, or how far she could trust me....

Six feet away two feds—their accents said Miami office—held the beams of flashlights on us, crossing like swords and piercing the darkness of our cover. In the side glow of the guy at right, I could make out a gun in his other hand.

And me still unarmed.

Every muscle in my body went hard except the part of me that *should* have been hard—Gaita and I had our clothes halfway off and lay entwined in what looked like a wild little sex party behind the packing crates only twenty feet away from the opening of an alley leading out of the area. And if that light hit me where I remained suspiciously limp, the flashlight guys might see I wasn't laying her, we were playing *them*....

It hadn't been my idea. Playing slightly inebriated lovers, we had flitted past the others stationed at strategic intervals; but these two held critical posts. I was all for charging them, knocking them over like bowling pins and taking a chance on the chase.

But Gaita had held me back.

"No," she whispered, insistent, "they will have guns."

"They won't get a chance to use them," I told her.

"Perhaps not. But if one discharged accidentally, the other militia, they would be alerted. And if they got to their feet while our backs were in view, then—"

"So I make sure they're taking a nice nap, after I lay 'em out on the pavement."

She shook her head, and dark curls bounced. "No, *señor*, two men with guns? No. If you fail, the game would be over."

My fists unbunched slowly. "Okay, sugar—but they're patrolling an area we can't get by without being seen. Let's hear your better idea...."

I caught the quick turn of her head in the darkness and

the flash of even, white teeth. "Perhaps you will even *like* it," she said.

I saw her hands move to the drawstring of the blouse by her throat. She moved one shoulder gently and let the dress fall away from her olive flesh. Then she reached behind my neck and pulled me down to the ground in a gentle spiral, took my hands, moved them to the swell of her naked breasts, at once soft and firm, and nestled me between silken bare legs while she busied her fingers with the zipper of my coveralls.

Her moan of delight came too soon and too loud and one leg thrashed out and kicked into something and—before I had a chance to move or even swear—her mouth closed on mine like a hungry trap, and I had a crazy instant of wondering what the hell I was doing here.

Under normal circumstances, I would have been hard as a rock with a vixen like this giving herself to me.

Under normal circumstances.

The flashlight beams lingered, then one snapped off and the guy behind it said, "Damn, they'll do it anywhere, these people."

Bare-breasted Gaita came out from under me, eyes wild and angry, nostrils flaring as she gave the two cops a Medusa stare, shrieking a stream of Spanish that was blistering even if you didn't understand it. It was the most beautiful response to getting caught in the act I ever saw.

And all I could do was try to readjust myself in the greasy coveralls.

For a second, light splashed my face as I tried to disappear inside the clothes, hoping the makeup and mustache wouldn't sweat off my face.

Gaita's act carried it, though.

The first one grunted, said, "Shut it, *muchacha*," then added, "Third pair of 'em tonight, and they all turn out the same way. The broad comes charging out like a tiger while the clown she's with just cowers like a kid caught stealing candy."

"These people," the other one said dismissively.

His partner paused, then made a motion with the light, streaking the darkness like a drunk guiding a plane in. "All right, you two—get your tails outa here and keep 'em covered. We got public decency laws in this country."

She spat at them and swore in her Cuban-dialect Spanish, and damned near kept it up too long. It was like she couldn't stop swearing and every once in a while something would come out in English.

Finally I grabbed her arm and dragged her out of there while she was aiming air kicks at their increasingly distant shins, and Shakespeare himself, writing a sequel to *The Taming of the Shrew*, couldn't have invented action any better suited to the scene.

Within minutes, we were outside their perimeter on a semi-darkened street, hugging the shadows while we headed west.

When I could, I said, "Fast thinking, *querida*."

"It was nothing." She sneered back at our long-gone audience. "It was what they expected and how they always react."

"It's always good when the other side underestimates you." I drew in some humid night air. "But we have another problem."

"*Señor?*"

"They may be bigots, but they aren't dopes. They'll report the incident or at least start thinking about it."

She frowned, considering that.

I went on: "I'm a lot bigger than your average Cuban, and that'll make me memorable. There's a sharp boy named Walter Crowley that these locals will report up the ladder to. He'll figure it out and widen the area of search."

After a moment, Gaita nodded and said, "It is most possible."

"It is most probable," I said.

Her face tilted up to mine and she gave me a peculiar glance. "But they do not have an army, *Señor* Morgan. This is a large city, Miami."

"They can *get* an army."

Her eyebrows lifted, casual yet serious. "In that case, *señor*, we must take the car."

"What car?"

"The one I have waiting, a block away. Where we go, they will not find you."

"You sound confident."

"That is because for such a place as I am taking you, many precautions must be taken for it to exist at all."

"It's your show," I said.

And so far, tonight, she'd been the star.

✿

The suite had an atmosphere about it, all right—nothing you could quite define, because the space was neither big nor elaborately furnished. But some thought had been given to it, a living room area, a bedroom, and a bathroom where I'd washed the makeup off, gotten out of the coveralls and taken a quick shower. Alone.

Now I sat in the big, comfortable chair with a cold can of beer in hand and gave my new surroundings some thought. It took a while, but it finally came to me.

This was a man's room, browns, yellows, tans, touches of black, furniture with strong simple lines suggesting strength but comfort…but a suite decorated by a woman *for* a man, with masculine comfort in mind, designed to instill male confidence.

Oh, there were enough feminine touches to inspire the beginnings of masculine passion, like the modern paintings that somehow suggested female figures, nude ones, with orange and red tones. From then on, comfort and confidence could take over.

Clothes had been waiting for me, and the sizes well estimated—a dark gray sport coat, black sport shirt, even darker gray slacks. I still had my own shoes and socks, but was damn glad to be rid of those lousy coveralls.

Still in her peasant blouse and skirt, Gaita sat at the dressing table, the stiff-bristled brush in her hand crackling through her lustrous hair, her eyes on me in the mirror while a faint smile played with the corners of her mouth.

"You are right, *Señor* Morgan. This is a *burdel*."

Whorehouse. Rose by any other name.

I took a pull of the beer. "I didn't say anything."

"Ah, but you have an awareness. It shows."

"Not on my face it doesn't."

"In your eyes, it does."

I let out a laugh. "Well, a bordello like this usually has out-of-the-way approaches. Like those damn alleys and tunnels we took to get here."

Her smile was a little too knowing. "You have been in other establishments like this before, *señor*?"

"Perhaps."

"...or perhaps not?"

"Really, no perhaps about it. Some of my best friends are *putas*."

For a second the brush paused in mid-stroke. "You do not seem like one who would need to make use of such facilities. To turn to the recourse of a woman who requires payment, this does not seem right."

I finished the beer. "I didn't say I paid any of them, kitten —but in my racket these places come in handy now and then. You can hide out in a whorehouse, because *nobody's* supposed to be there."

"Well put, Morgan. A most intelligent answer."

"Must come from having damn near a complete college education." I grinned at her. "Ask anybody—I'm an intelligent guy...in some ways."

One eyebrow arched though both eyes were half lidded. "Could not such intelligence have been put to better use?"

"Not by me. I'm one of those guys born in the wrong era that you hear about. Baby, I wasn't made for this world."

"Possibly it wasn't made for you either."

"I get by."

"Do you?" She put the brush down and stood abruptly, still facing the mirror, hands on her hips, legs apart, then took a deep breath. "You seem relaxed for what you have been through in recent days. Almost...placid. Why is that, *Señor* Morgan?"

"Just 'Morgan,' *querida*. Why *not* be relaxed? I'm not going anywhere—not until you tell me the score."

Gently, she pivoted like a dancer to face me. "Those who look for you...they will be here. They will know of this place. Perhaps some have been patrons."

I frowned. "Yeah?"

"But they will not find you. Fortunately for your sake, this is the...house *extraordinario*."

"Delicate way to refer to a whorehouse," I said.

"Our clientele appreciates that it is so." She looked at me, and when I stayed quiet, she said, "It is surprising how many men of stature in business and government prefer private, uh...*outlets* for certain personal activities beyond the doors of their own homes."

"It's an old story, kid."

"It is also an old story that such men often seem to prefer women who are not so pale of skin, nor skinny, nor fat. Behind closed doors, with these strange dark women..." Her tone was arch now, her smile wicked, mocking. "...such men can shed the sexual inhibitions of modern civilization that they find so limiting to their pleasures."

My eyebrows had long since hiked in surprise.

She noticed that, and nodded. "Yes, *señor*, I too have studied in the college. The university. Does this surprise you?"

"Not anymore it doesn't."

"But there is learning, *señor*," she said, "and then there is *learning*."

Gaita walked to the carved oak bar in the corner, poured herself a finger of rum, and tossed it down like a thirsty sailor. "This place is, in itself, the university. The pupils learn, but the instructors, they do not *realize* they instruct."

I wasn't sure I was following her. Curiouser and curiouser, as Alice said.

"The world is in a state of, how do you say it? Flux. Of change. There is much trouble ahead. Not long ago, my people were promised that Castro would be gone and Cuba ours again—then your president was shot like a dog in the street, and where are our dreams now?"

I shrugged. "Your people had the CIA and the Mob and everybody else helping you, not long ago. But those days are over."

"Perhaps. But the struggle goes on. And men in your government, when they come to this place that they find so enjoyable, *they* are the instructors. The…" She searched for just the right word. "…the *unwitting* instructors."

"Pillow talk," I said, smiling a little, getting it now.

She smiled back, drifting nearer where I sat. "And we are the ones who learn, and who pass *what* we learn along to those who can use it most profitably."

"Nice," I said. "So who gets squeezed in the middle?"

"You do not yet understand." She sucked in her breath and began to prowl the room, as cat-like as her name promised, touching decorative items idly along the way. "We are *pro*-American, but for *all* the Americas."

"Then you have others besides U.S. citizens on your client list?"

"Naturally." She turned, smiling again. "Many men from below the border have a passion for your pale blonde women. This...*type* also has a place here in this house. It is very profitable."

"I would imagine."

Her hair tossed as she slowly shook her head. "By profitable, I do not mean in the monetary sense...at least not primarily."

This was a whorehouse dealing in state secrets and probably blackmail, and the money the girls made was only incidental.

I leaned back in the chair and opened the other beer she had set out. "Sooner or later you're going to get to the point, honey."

Her laugh was sudden and low, but with a lilt to it. "We have a quarry, one Jaimie Halaquez, who must be found. It is a matter of necessity and pride and as an example that will prove a deterrent for others in the future." She stopped, her mouth pursed. "The trail to *Señor* Halaquez is not so obscure as you might think."

"Really?"

"Oh yes. *Señor* Halaquez was a frequent guest here, and as such, certain things were learned about him. Not *from* him as much as *about* him. In retrospect, we should not have been surprised by his betrayal."

"Pedro said it was a complete surprise."

She sighed. "We knew that Halaquez was a traitor by definition—after all, he worked for Castro, took money from that regime, and yet he helped us. This blinded us to his most obvious trait."

"That his chief loyalty was to himself."

"*Si, señor.*"

I smirked at her. "You really couldn't have stopped him?"

"For over a year he lay in wait. Then he moved quickly. He had to. My people have a vengeful nature."

I nodded. "Do you have him located?"

"Not yet. But we do know where he *has* been, and one other thing—and this, *señor*, is *most* important—we know the single weakness that will trap him eventually."

I leaned forward, the beer almost forgotten. "What?"

"His thirst for sexual gratification," Gaita said. "His vanity and his physical need for a woman. Not just *any* woman, Morgan—only the most beautiful will do."

"So what's his kink?" Sounded like a game show.

"His tastes run to the...rough. He likes them young, but he also likes a woman of experience—any woman older than thirteen and younger than fifty, if she is beautiful and willing to...to play his sick games."

An S & M freak. Hell, it was a place to start.

She looked at me for a long moment. "With just that one thing, you should be able to find him."

"If it's that easy, why don't you just run him down yourself?"

Gaita's face was absolutely impassive, but there was a strange expression in her eyes.

"Because, Morgan, he is a totally deadly person—a ruthless man trained to kill, who *enjoys* killing...and is more than the match for anyone we might send after him."

Well, maybe not anyone....

She went on: "We have many who have volunteered for the mission, but these are brave Cuban boys we cannot afford to lose—young men of bravery but who were...what is the expression? In water over their heads."

"But you're okay risking a *gringo*'s life?"

"That is not fair, *señor*." Her expression turned grave. "Three who took the assignment on their own initiative were successful enough to locate him, only to die painfully for their efforts. Slow deaths, *señor*. With a knife. Here."

She touched her belly.

"Since then," she said, "we have discouraged any such attempts. All those three succeeded in doing was to warn *Señor* Halaquez...and now he will be more wary than ever."

I drank half the beer and put the can down. "He's only safe with the money when he gets to Cuba. You don't head west to get there. He could go south and try to cut across from Mexico, but my bet is you have pipelines into there, too, and he'd be picked up or your people alerted."

She nodded.

"He wouldn't chance getting caught in open country by somebody with a rifle, so he'd have to stay where any hostile contact would be made personally, so he could handle it, and that would mean sticking to the cities, and those Mexican cities sure wouldn't be friendly to him at all. If he went north, his only available exit points would be international ports, and even there your people and sympathizers might lay hands on him."

She nodded again, slowly. "*Where* then, Morgan?"

"Right here in his own back yard," I said, "where he has previously established contacts. He's close to Cuba, if he can make escape arrangements, he knows the area, and the probable moves of your organization…and all he has to do is wait for the right time and place to skip on out. Do you have any theory about why he hasn't already skipped?"

"We do not."

"I do. He needs to launder that money—well, not launder it, exactly. He'll need to get it exchanged for currency that's legal in Cuba—money from a country with normalized relations."

"Would that be difficult for him?"

"No, but he would likely go through underground channels. And because he's keeping his head down, he's probably using middlemen. That may give me a lead on him. It's the one thing that would force him out of hiding."

Her eyes tightened. "Unless…"

"Unless what?"

"His own lust for the perverted sex, that may also…as you say, force him out."

I looked around the room. "Well, he's not coming here."

"No. But there are other such places. And there is one other possibility."

"Yeah?"

"When he learns, *señor*, that one capable of matching his skills is hunting him down? He may come after you. The hunted may prefer to become the hunter."

I snorted a laugh. "So *that's* how I got picked for the job. You fine folks want me to do the flush job."

She shrugged, smiled just a little. "It was you who volunteered, *Señor* Morgan."

I picked up the beer, finished it and leaned back again. "Hell, kid, I'm not complaining. Everything was getting too damn dull anyway. I was getting stale. I can use a break in the routine, to pick up my thinking again."

She stood there in front of me, that enigmatic smile playing with the corners of her mouth again. Her hand went up to her throat, her fingers wove inside the drawstring of the blouse, and this time when she moved her shoulders the blouse came slipping off to her waist and she was like one of those bare-breasted Tahitian natives Gauguin loved to paint.

Once again her hands and arms moved, flowing behind her with swift, definite purpose, then the full skirt fell, taking the blouse with it, a fabric waterfall that pooled around her feet and she was a naked, lovely thing with olive skin that had a sheen to it and midnight hair that ornamented her to perfection. She pulled down white panties to fully reveal the dark delta that had already been showing through, and she kicked them away.

"You can have me, *Señor* Morgan, for a…break in your routine."

"But I won't," I said.

Her eyes changed again. Surprise. Disappointment? "Why, Morgan?"

"I don't like to be tested, baby."

She luxuriated in an animal-like stretch, her lips opening in a smile, her pelvis jutting forward sensuously, the sucked-in breath lifting her breasts even higher until she looked more like an artist's conception than the living, vital thing she was. The expression in her eyes was clear now. It was one of relief.

She let her breath out slowly, a look of pleasure crossing her face. "Yes, *Señor* Morgan. You *are* man enough to take Jaimie Halaquez. He could not stand before you."

I saw the tip of her tongue dart pinkly between her teeth. "And now since you have passed the test...you may *really* have me, if you wish. Not as a reward or a bribe or even a gesture of thanks. But because I *want* you to."

And it wasn't an act this time.

My throat felt tight. "Honey," I said, "haven't you heard? I'm a married man...."

Her eyes didn't leave mine. Something seemed to satisfy her at last, because she still smiled and the pleasure remained in her face. "Your wife must be a very special woman."

"I haven't seen her for a year. If we're both lucky, I'll never see her again."

She frowned. "I do not understand."

"Not sure I do either, kid."

Her head went back. Her breasts jutted. And this time, if those feds had flashed a light on me, I'd have been hard enough to pass the audition.

"A man of such determination I must kiss," she said. "That you cannot refuse me. A woman's heart is pleased that such men still exist."

I couldn't have stopped her if I'd wanted to.

She stepped out of the pile of clothes and walked toward me, exhilarating in her nakedness, the constant challenge apparent in the subtle, eager flexing of the muscles that played under that soft olive flesh. She reached down, tilted my chin up, then bent at the waist and let her mouth brush mine softly, the wish plain behind the lush dampness, but no insistent demand at all. Inadvertently, my fingertips brushed the firm texture of her thigh, then I drew them back and she stood.

"I could love you, Morgan."

"Not a good idea."

"You are right. I should not fall into a trap that you do not wish to set."

She walked away and stood in front of the mirror over the dressing table, studying me in the glass. Her rump was a rounded, dimpled distraction.

"What is it you *do* want, Morgan? There are things I could do for you, *to* you, that may not violate your quaint morality. Tell me, and whatever it is I will give it to you."

"A gun," I said. "Standard Army issue Colt .45 automatic."

Her eyes laughed at me. "That is all?"

"For now," I said. "So put your clothes on and fill me in."

Watching her go through the measured motions of dressing was even more torturous than seeing her strip. Everything she did now appeared unconsciously exciting, and I couldn't stop looking at her.

You could die tomorrow, man, a voice was saying. *Hell, you could die tonight. And you don't want to say yes to this finely stacked beauty?*

Maybe she didn't mean to tempt me. *Right.* She *had* to be deliberately tantalizing about the whole process or she wouldn't have been a woman. When they have you in a bind, they like to put the screws to you all the way.

When she was done, she smiled gently at me and said, "You really *could* have taken advantage of me, *Señor* Morgan. But I do think morality becomes you."

"I was just thinking it's a pain in the ass," I said. "Now fill me in some more on this operation you have working here."

"Gladly, *Señor* Morgan. What you have seen up to this point was simply an emergency route, if there was ever necessity to make a quick and safe exit. It leads only to this room."

These were very special quarters, then—a sort of hotel suite-style safe house.

"I assure you," she was saying, "that the remainder of the premises are much more elaborate, and more varied in their escape possibilities."

"Well, you never know when you're going to have to make a fast exit out of a whorehouse."

That actually got a little laugh out of her. She gestured. "Come, there are others waiting to meet you…and I can give you a glimpse of what *else* is on offer here.…"

CHAPTER FOUR

Gaita's brief description of the establishment was much too modest.

From selected apertures at strategic locations, I was able to see the plush bar and tap room, a polished mahogany restoration of the gilt-edged 1900s. There was a casino adjoining with a Vegas-like array of gaming and a small stage at one end, and buffet tables against two walls, prime rib and cracked crab and all sorts of goodies for patrons who had worked up an appetite, presumably having sated other appetites they'd brought with them.

The dark-haired Cuban cutie pointed out tactfully concealed entrances to the upstairs rooms where customers could discreetly avail themselves of certain services. And everything was modernized now—no such thing as cash anymore, this was strictly a credit card business with coded statements at addresses or post office boxes of the client's choice. Those enjoying the facilities were carefully screened before admittance, vouched for and vetted and to date there had been no police intervention at all.

It took longer than it should have, but finally it hit me.

I was inside the notorious Mandor Club, that ultra-select bordello whose existence was whispered about in elite circles and known to but a few.

I had stumbled across the name ten years earlier, in Rio, when a lovely-but-been-around redhead had invited me out on a cruise on her yacht, which she hadn't obtained by selling Girl Scout Cookies door to door. She'd been great company and a memorable lay, but had become a little maudlin half-way through a magnum of champagne and damn near told me the story of her life, whether I wanted to hear it or not.

Four years as a Mandor Club hostess had set the redhead up in luxury for life, but the stipulation was that she retire outside the United States, a requirement for all of the club's retirees. Giddy or not, she realized fairly deep in her tale that she'd spilled too much, got a little pale, spilled some more over the rail of the boat, then said no more on the subject of one of the world's greatest whorehouses.

"Well laid out," I told Gaita, "if you'll pardon the expression."

A smile twitched the lush lips. "A grand old dream of a grand old man...long dead." She gestured like a guide on a palace tour. "The building itself was once a mansion, surrounded by others of its kind, but over the years people of wealth moved to other places, and many of the structures were brought down. This fine old place, sitting back on generous grounds, was in a good position for new owners to... conduct business."

"You're not talking about last week."

"No. More like...last century."

I gazed down at the floor again where several beautiful women in tasteful if low-cut evening dress had gathered, preparing for a cheerful night's debauch. They were Latin, they were Asian, they were black, they were white. I might have to revise my opinion of the United Nations.

I asked, "Who runs the joint *this* century, *querida*?"

"You are about to meet her." Gaita took my arm. "This way please, *señor*."

A door activated by a buzzer from the interior opened onto a room as functionally modern as an insurance company office. Business machines were beside the two empty desks, filing cabinets lined the walls, a new, formidable-looking vault dominated the rear, and the only decorative concessions to the nature of this business were two oil-painting nudes by a world-famous pin-up artist in elaborate gilt frames, and a leather couch beside a paisley wall hanging.

Beneath the paintings, at a gray, glass-topped steel desk, sat a woman of almost timeless beauty, fingering the neckline of a sleek black dress, then idly running her fingers through piled-high blonde hair with weird purple highlights. This stunning, mature beauty was slowly scanning the pages of a ledger.

Her birth name had been Louise Cader Gibbs. Her husband had died in a federal prison ten years ago, early in a term resulting from a stock market scandal that had turned Wall Street upside down and sideways. She hadn't looked up yet, so she didn't see me grinning.

I said, "Hell, Bunny, you *do* bounce back, don't you?"

Then her eyes rose to mine, and hit with the force of a punch. Her face went through a strange transformation as a montage of reminiscences played in her brain and reflected out her eyes.

Finally she chuckled deep in her throat. "Damn," she said. "Morgan the Raider. The only son of a bitch who ever managed to take that old fox I married for a hunk of his ill-acquired fortune."

"It's what I do," I said with a shrug. "Or anyway, what I used to do."

Gaita was looking quizzically at us both. "Madam...I am not surprised you know *of* Morgan...but you *know* Morgan?"

Bunny sat back and relished the moment, then rose and walked over to me with her hand outstretched. "Know him? Honey, I once paid out a contract to have him killed." Her hand was strong and warm in mine. "Remember that, Morgan?"

"Rings a bell."

"But..." Gaita smiled. "...he does not seem to be dead, Madam."

Bunny laughed that deep laugh again and shook her head. "No, but two times, guys supposed to do the job were found *completely* dead. And seemed nobody wanted to pick up my contract after that."

"Can I help it," I said, "that you hired accident-prone types?"

"Anybody who takes you on, Morgan, is an accident waiting to happen."

"Still sore?"

"Hell no, Morgan! A major rule of business is knowing when not to throw good money after bad....I wrote it off as a loss. Even found a way to deduct it off my taxes that year."

"Must have been interesting wording on that tax form."

She gestured to a chair and I sat, while she perched nearby on the edge of her desk. A lot of leg showed, thanks to a slit in the black dress—nicely rounded gams, more substantial than the Twiggy types, and fine by me.

"Sure burned my husband's heinie, though," she said with a chuckle. "He bitched about not getting even with you till the day he died—indignant to the end...and with all the people *he* screwed over, who never got even with *him*!"

"We all see the world through our end of the telescope, Bunny."

She shook her head. Great smile on the gal, lots of white teeth that were maybe even hers. "What did you ever do with that dough? Better than half a *million* you nipped us for. And that was back when half a mil was money."

"Well, I saw some of the world I hadn't seen so far. You know me and boats." I leaned back and gave her the once-over. "You look pretty damn good, Bunny. Don't you know madams aren't supposed to look better than their girls? Crazy hair, though."

She touched a purple streak. "Sets me off from those girls. Like the man says, a madam has to *look* like a madam, otherwise she'd disappoint the customers." She paused and laughed again. "Anyway, I'm not fool enough to believe I can compete with my girls." She touched her generous bosom. "This chick has got some miles on her...but at least I found my level."

"What happened to high society?"

She snorted a laugh. "The *grande dames* booted me out ...and now I socialize more with their husbands than I ever did with them. As a matter of fact, I've begun to think I've found the profession I was truly cut out for. The old fox knew what he was doing when he bought this place back when he had the bread…this was the only investment we hung onto! So don't feel sorry for me."

"Never that, Bunny."

She stared at me, as if through new eyes. "So *you're* the one that got the mission," she mused. "I didn't know *who* it would be."

"You're playing kind of funny games, aren't you, Bunny? Traveling in strange circles?"

Her smile turned sideways. "That makes two of us, doesn't it?"

"I could expect it of me."

"But not of me, eh? Well, my old friend, don't fool yourself. Times have changed, people change with them. I'm here, where I am accepted, instead of castigated, and I have good friends in strange places. Anyway, the old fox and I had investments in Cuba that we lost when that bearded bum took over."

I grinned big. "Ah. So there lies the source of your Cuban exile sympathies."

"They're nice people, and I don't like to see nice people get hurt." She reached out and squeezed my arm. "I'm glad it's you, Morgan. It'll take a man like you to take Jaimie Halaquez down. I'm going to follow this with pleasure." She tossed a thumb at Gaita, who had melted back into the periphery. "They've assigned you a good one." Then to Gaita, "Do you have everything ready?"

"For this evening, madam? Yes."

"Good. Then take Morgan back to your room and keep him out of sight until it's time. He'll need a lot of filling in."

I sat forward. "This little kitten's already done a good share of filling me in. But you could do some more."

Bunny's eyebrows rose. "Oh?"

"What can you tell me about Halaquez?"

The madam was frowning. "What has Gaita told you?"

"That he was a patron here. That he's a ruthless killer with sadistic tastes that bleed over into his sexual kinks."

Her laugh held a hollow ring. "Well, Morg, you seem to know the score already."

I shook my head. "I need to *really* know this bastard if I'm going to track him. Get specific, doll."

She frowned. Mentally, she sorted through file cards, selecting just the right facts, just the right words. "He's an odd one, even for a customer into bondage and discipline. He wants the shame of it, even to torture. His needs extend well beyond what we provide here at Mandor."

"Such as?"

"The lash."

My jaw damn near dropped. "He wants to be whipped?"

"Yes. But that is not why we came to forbid him from our doors."

"You *banned* his ass?"

She nodded. "The game of submission is such that there are guidelines—lines that don't get crossed, code words agreed upon to stop the game. But he would push the women hired to dominate him—beg them for more."

"More torture?"

"More pain. Yes."

I thought about it. "Okay. So the idiot wants his ass whipped. Whip it, and take his credit card number. Why not?"

"If only it were that simple." Bunny glanced at Gaita, whose head was lowered. "When the game was over, when the girl had done whatever he asked…he would pay, as required, he would even provide a handsome tip. But on occasion…not every time, perhaps once every three visits, then later on, after every other visit…he would punish the girl."

Frowning, I said, "I thought these freaks *liked* being dominated."

"Oh, they do. But when the game is over, some feel shame, and a sado-masochistic bastard like Halaquez will suddenly take it out on the very person he hired to humiliate him."

I shook my head; my belly was tight with disgust. "Getting even for indignities he'd paid to have done to him. Man. This is one sick puppy."

"Yes," Bunny said. "Someone should put him out of his misery."

"But this is great," I said, beaming at her.

"Great?"

"Now we have a lead. Now we know how he gets his jollies, and it's from a menu served up at a limited number of venues. You must know other houses or girls working solo, doing the S & M thing. It's a way to find him."

Bunny's eyes were tight. "I think you will find Mr. Halaquez is banned from all such establishments, and the word's gotten around among the women who work the bondage trade out of their apartments, as well. But I will give you a list, if you think that may help."

"Sure. It's a start."

"The only other thing, Morgan…but it's a long shot."

"Hell. Guys get rich playing long shots. Go."

Again she chose her words carefully. "There is a rumor… and for now it's *just* a rumor…that the Consummata is setting up shop in Miami."

I blinked. "Who or what is the 'Consummata'?"

"A very famous *dominatrix*, at least famous in certain circles."

"From Miami?"

"From nowhere. From everywhere. Sometimes she works alone, by appointment through intermediaries. Other times she has set up a location with other young women trained in the arts of sado-masochism. And, again, clients are by referral only. She has turned up in every major city in America and not a few in Europe. Her clients, they say, are among the most rich and powerful men in business and government. *If* she exists."

"You don't even know if she exists?"

"She is a rumor. A wisp of smoke. A legend. A dream. Lovely, a vision in black leather, they say…and, brother, would I hire her for the Mandor in a heartbeat."

"How do I find her?"

Her laugh was inaudible. "I don't think you can. But I can put the word out. If Jaimie Halaquez hears that the Consummata has graced Miami with her presence, he will certainly try to make an appointment with her. Any concerns for his safety, anything smacking of common sense, will fly from his evil mind."

"Consummata," I said, tasting the word. "What is that? Spanish? Italian?"

"Latin," Gaita chimed in from the sidelines. "It has several meanings. One is…crowning touch. The other you might guess."

"Sexual consummation," I said.

"Got it in one," Bunny said, cheerfully, slipping off her desk onto her feet.

I got up and faced her. "You've been a big help, kiddo."

"Oh, you'll be seeing more of me, Morgan."

"You sure you really *want* that?"

She laughed. "Not sure at all. You might get ideas about raiding *me*. I wouldn't put it past you…though why, with forty million bucks stashed away, you'd want to bother with small change like little ol' me, I'd never know."

"Don't believe everything you read in the papers, Bunny."

"About you, Morgan?" She slipped an arm in mine, walking me to the door. "I'd believe anything."

Jaimie Halaquez had gone on the run with a purpose in mind.

He had tested the defenses and offensive capabilities of the opposition, and found them lacking in strength. His first kill had been made in a small motel outside of St. Louis, a young Cuban who'd been smart enough to find Halaquez but not skilled enough to survive. The next contact had been made north of Little Rock, and a third near

77

Meridian, Mississippi, both resulting in dead emissaries from Miami's Cuban community.

Traced on a map, Halaquez's path took him away from the Miami area, then swung him back toward it again. These movements had nothing to do with reaching his final destination.

But wherever he was now, he was in position to make that final move.

The only thing that had me wondering was the relatively small amount of money involved. To some people—like those he'd taken it from—seventy-five thousand bucks was a lot of loot. If Halaquez made it to Cuba, and the dough had been converted properly, it could mean a lot more. Still, the Cuban exiles were, in their way, a national political group, and taking them on for this kind of cash was asking for trouble. Almost stupidly so.

And even if Halaquez did make it to Cuba, with the cash converted to a friendly-to-Cuba country's currency, there would still be anti-Castro sympathizers ready to cut him down the first chance they got, and seventy-five grand wasn't about to buy him perpetual protection.

A funny little hunch was scratching at me again. From one angle, this seemed all cut-and-dry, but from another it was sticky and wet. This was feeling like much more than just a small-time heist of $75,000 made worse by the betrayal it represented; to the Cubans of Little Havana, this seemed like a very big deal, but the reality was, the Halaquez score was small change.

So why did it feel *like the big time?*

Something seemed to be missing from the equation, and the longer I thought about it, the more that seemed to be the case. Offhand, it might look like a quick grab for seventy-five thousand bucks, and that could be enough of an incentive for anybody, even an amateur.

But then amateurs would hesitate at pulling off three kills, any one of which might get botched, risking Jaimie getting his ass slammed in some local jail. Halaquez could have disappeared into the vastness of America and somehow made it to Canada or Mexico, and become just another Latin louse with a grubstake. Instead, he'd hopscotched his way back to the Miami area....

Jaimie Halaquez had stolen money and left the state, and committed a trio of murders along the way, making this now an interstate affair, which meant the Feds were onboard. The FBI would have its ears to the ground and its own contacts within the Cuban freedom organization, so they'd know, at least basically, what was going on.

Whatever Halaquez was up to, it had all the earmarks of big professionalism, and the big pros don't make a Federal case out of seventy-five thousand bucks.

I sat there in a Mandor suite decorated with an oriental motif, feeling ill at ease and even silly in a business suit padded out to make me look like a pudgy city councilman, hair powdered gray, and in pinched shoes that made my steps mince because I couldn't help it.

The only thing that lent any comfort was the weight of the .45 in my belt and the three spare clips in my pocket.

Tami, a lush blonde who could have stepped out of the

centerfold of the highest-end men's magazine, kept looking at me through heavily made-up eyes that she kept half-lowered in deliberate fashion.

"Tell me, Morgan, if this were real life…would a girl like me *really* be attracted enough to a man like you to make her want to marry him?"

By "a man like you," Tami meant the pudgy councilman I was pretending to be.

"If I were rich enough," I said.

"Is that the only reason?"

I squirmed under the dark suit jacket. "Could be gratitude by way of blackmail. A guy like 'me' could have kept your sweet behind out of a jail cell."

Long eyelashes, not real but pretty enough, fluttered. "What would it take for a man like the *real* you to be attracted to a girl like me?"

"Not much. You have it all going for you, sugar. But you need to know something…"

"You don't pay."

"Bingo."

The living wet dream squirmed, looking at Gaita. "The man has confidence," she remarked casually.

"Didn't mean to hit a nerve," I said.

"Oh, you didn't."

Gaita snapped her fingers abruptly at both of us. "Please! Now is not the time for such nonsense." To the blonde, she asked, "You are sure about what you must do?"

Tami nodded. "Mr. Boyer is drunk again, and I'm little Tessie, come to drag him out of the house of ill repute."

"Always liked that phrase," I said with a half a smile.

The lovely whore, dressed to pass as a rich man's wife, continued: "The chauffeur downstairs will see it all, discreetly turn away, and have something to talk about at the next card game among Mr. Boyer's male staff."

Gaita, doggedly serious, said to the girl, "And then?"

"And then delivery to the Amherst Hotel, where our friend gives Mr. Boyer's clothes back to me, while I return to home base in time to get the real Boyer back into his clothes, and smuggle the old boy out…and hope nobody notices the time discrepancy."

I said, "Suppose we get stopped along the way?"

"Our tough luck," Tami told me. "You'll have to deal with it."

"I will," I said.

Gaita checked her watch. "It is eleven o'clock. You leave now."

Time had worked in my favor.

The local police had long since vanished back to their regular assignments, and Walter Crowley's men had thinned down to a few spot checkers who were still working areas where they thought I might be hiding.

I grinned to myself when I thought of Crowley sitting someplace, fuming. He'd have that receipt for my body, dead or alive, tucked away in his wallet, and every minute I was on the loose increased my chances of being taken back dead. Much as he might relish delivering me without a pulse, he would surely much prefer to deliver me breathing, and with the possibility of finding that forty mil.

Hell, if I had any sense of humor at all, I would send

Crowley a letter telling him just where that pile of dough was, or anyway where the guy who put it there *said* it was. According to the raider who had framed *this* Morgan, the forty mil was right where my namesake, Sir Henry Morgan the Pirate, put his treasure.

Well, buddy, I told Crowley in my head, *lots of luck —just try and find it.*

Everybody else had, and failed. Old Morgan operated out of Cuban waters with a preference for the island of Santa Catalina, and all the reference works were easily accessible in the public library, or in certain archives for more rarified researchers, with plenty of folklore and rumors to keep treasure hunters hopping every year.

But on the Nuevo Cadiz mission, Morgan the Raider had been raided. One of the five men who had made up my crew in the war—when we took down those two armored cars and created the template for the money-truck heist—had been "vacationing" on that island, trying to make a deal with the government for laundering the loot. And I had turned up unexpectedly in his midst.

He was dead now, my old friend, his head blasted apart like a melon by my .45 slug, and any further details about exactly where the forty mil was stashed had gone away in a spray of gore.

Maybe my old friend *had* found one of Morgan's places of safekeeping. One thing, that hiding place—whether in a cave or some old building or the remnants thereof—had most certainly been found after all these years, considering how many treasure hunters had gone looking. Surely it had been empty when my pal found it. *Somebody* would have been there long before him....

And once my pal stowed the forty mil there, anybody searching for the first Morgan's treasure might have already have stumbled onto *Morgan the Raider's* treasure—the treasure that could clear my name.

Meaning that place of safekeeping might be empty again. People just don't pass up forty million in beautiful U.S. currency.

At least my pal would never spend another dime of it. My old buddy was good and goddamn dead, but if he only knew what was going down now for *his* old buddy, he'd be laughing his balls off, because my army buddy had wanted me dead in the worst way. He tried to make it happen several times... only I got him first.

How'd you work it, Old Buddy? Like Hitler? Ol' Shicklgruber had his submarines booby-trapped, so that no matter how many years after they were sunk, nobody dared touch them, because they'd blow up in their faces. They were still at the bottom, prizes of war, their locations marked SECRET and left alone for the sea to swallow in due course of time, maybe with a minor upheaval and some surface turbulence when one blew; but with nobody around to get hurt, at least. You do it that way, pal? When I finally find the loot, will it blow up in my puss? Did you...?

"Morgan!" Gaita's voice had a sharp ring to it, cutting through my thoughts. "We are ready."

I stood, uncomfortable in my clothes. "Sorry, kid. Just reflecting."

"At the wrong time, such reflection, it can get you killed."

"So can not reflecting at all," I advised her.

The briefing they had given me on the real Boyer covered him being a professional politician from an upstate county, a pol known for his indiscretions and peccadillos, but with enough votes in his pocket to keep him affluent. His sexual preference was young, dark-skinned girls, preferably of Latin ancestry, and he frequently visited Miami to patronize establishments that catered to his special tastes…and his former showgirl wife was known to just as frequently have to haul his drunken tail out of said establishments.

The real Mrs. Boyer was more than a little protective of her current position in life, afraid that she might lose that position to some enterprising sexpot who could cut the pudgy pol loose from any family ties the way the current Mrs. Boyer had the former Mrs. Boyer.

Apparently the woman had gone to certain lengths to avoid anybody recognizing her on these missions of wifely mercy, staying swathed in veils and always coming in a taxi; but her blonde hair and stripper's body had always given her away. Not much of a disguise was required for Tami to fit the role.

The taxi was supplied by a friendly Cuban exile driver. I played my part with my head down, doing a stumbling drunk act, careful to keep my face averted to avoid more than a casual scrutiny. Tami did the rest, and nobody paid any attention to us.

Luck was on my side again: we made our exit on a night when the Mandor had a particularly high-profile clientele in the house. If the cops had elected to pull a raid, they would have had one hell of a time in court, trying hard to find a judge who wouldn't have to disqualify himself as a friend and associate of any of these potential defendants.

Already the thing was almost put over. The taxi cut through the streets, heading toward the western section of town, and for some reason I got that funny feeling again. A long time ago I learned not to ignore it—a tightness at the back of my neck, and a clammy feeling there, my jaws clamped so tight, any more pressure would chip my teeth.

It wasn't intuition. Not exactly. And it wasn't fear or nervousness. It was just this *thing* that had become my best friend.

Call it instinct, or maybe luck again, whispering in my ear like a tender lover.

I said, "Pull over at the corner."

The driver nodded and began slowing down, edging toward the curb.

Tami looked at me curiously and said, "But we're not near the Amherst Hotel yet."

"I know. But I get out here."

"That is *not* the plan."

"I *know*, kid. But I get out here—okay?"

She swallowed. Nodded. "What about the clothes?"

Even while she was saying it, I was busy shucking off the coat and pants that had been liberated off the doped-up politician. I got into the stuff Gaita had bought for me, the same gray jacket, black sport shirt and gray slacks, and I made sure the .45 was in place in my waistband.

Then I told the driver to take Tami and his heap back to where he had picked us up.

The hooker's face in the rear window was tense with worry, her fingers splayed against the glass. I blew her a kiss that got a tiny smile out of her.

Then I walked the other eight blocks.

As I came around the corner, I got a great view of a pyrotechnics display that must have rivaled anything Miami pulled off on July Fourth.

I flinched, but that was all, as I watched the nearest side of the Hotel Amherst blow apart in a shower of brick and glass that decorated a huge orange ball of flame and billows of charcoal smoke.

Cars screeched to a stop, some pedestrians froze and screamed and others ran and yelled, and I moved through them toward the hotel like a sleepwalker, stepping over burning rubble. Sirens were just kicking in as I entered the building.

Not much later, I learned that four people had died in the explosion, and that room 409—where I had reservations under the name of R. Sinclair—had disintegrated.

What the hell. I decided to check in, anyway.

Surely they had other rooms available.

CHAPTER FIVE

The lobby had only the faintest tinge of smoke, the explosion happening several floors up and on the other side of the building.

I had to stand in line behind flustered, frightened guests who were hurriedly checking out, businessmen mostly but a few couples, hauling their own luggage. I carried an empty suitcase that had contained the change of clothes I was wearing now. The process was slow, because a guest inventory was under way, which would be tricky to execute, because anybody who happened to be out for the evening would start out on the M.I.A. list.

A frazzled-looking group of guests who apparently hadn't decided to check out (at least not yet), some in bathrobes, all with wild eyes, were clustered among the plump chairs and potted ferns while a female hotel staffer threaded through, checking their names off a list.

The missing would not include the Mr. Sinclair who was supposed to have occupied the room, because he hadn't checked in yet. And nobody would blame him, either, for taking one look at the smoke-bleeding Hotel Amherst and turning around to go looking for another place to stay.

Checking in, I of course did not use the name R. Sinclair.

I took a room on the first floor under H. Moran, figuring if anybody really wanted to find me, the initials and the

Morgan–Moran similarity would make it easy for them—friend or foe. After all, why hide?

Somebody had been on to our arrangements. Somebody knew what time I was expected to check in, and had made all the preparations for my arrival, and they hadn't left a fruit basket. Firemen were moving through the lobby, their chatter indicating they were processing an apparent gas explosion. But I figured it was a time bomb set-up.

The firefighters let it slip, as they spoke among themselves, that so far four bodies had been located. Four people dead, casually murdered, in the failed attempt to remove me. Collateral damage, the military called it. I wouldn't forget that four strangers lost their lives for my sake. They hadn't done so willingly, their sacrifice had been thrust upon them, but I would avenge them just the same.

The owner of the place, a small bald mustached fellow with a calm his staffers might well envy, had taken over the desk.

"As you can see, Mr. Moran," he said with admirable professionalism, "we are mostly checking guests *out*, not in. Are you quite certain you want to stay with us? I have no way to tell what kind of inconveniences you may face."

"Have the fire department boys said you have to shut down? That you're not to take any new guests?"

"Well, no...."

"Then I'm going to assume my money is as good as the next guy's."

I said that in a friendly way, and his smile was friendly back at me.

"You're welcome to stay with us, though I can't imagine

why under these circumstances you would want to."

But I was already signing in. "Hell, friend, I'll see worse places tomorrow."

"Really?" Just a polite response, but with some curiosity in it, too.

"Yeah. My business is snatching up crappy blocks of buildings for a song, and then holding them until the government shells out for urban renewal projects. This is the closest lodging to where I want to prowl around."

That was enough to get his attention, and explain my unlikely preference for this hotel. He'd remember my cover story, I knew, because I noted his shrewd look as he studied me. *Maybe* he *could be part of the next buying parcel*, he was thinking.

I was almost home free, but a fire inspector—he wore a fireman's helmet and a plainclothes cop's business suit—caught the tail end of me checking in, and came over to give me a hard time.

"You don't want to be checking in here," he said. He was big and blond and about fifty, with shaggy eyebrows as out of control as the worst fire he ever investigated.

"Actually, I do," I said. "I have business near here tomorrow, and there are plenty of undamaged rooms available, well away from what you fellas are looking into."

He said he thought I was nuts, and called over a tall, thin cop he called Homer. They talked about me while I stood there placidly, hoping nobody asked me for the I.D. I didn't have, and that the .45 in my waistband under the gray sport jacket wasn't bulging at all.

Then the fire inspector trotted off to handle something more important, while Homer the cop said in a high, husky voice, "Buddy, this place is liable to be closed officially pretty soon."

"Tonight?"

"No, but by tomorrow maybe."

I picked up my empty suitcase and looked at him. "Friend," I said, "where else is there around here to go right now?"

"Sir...." His voice was pleasant. Too damn pleasant. "There are *plenty* of other hotels."

"In season and right now, without reservations?"

"So maybe you'll have to look around a little."

"How much got busted out by the blast?"

"Quite a bit."

"But not in the wing I'm in." I gave him a big boys-will-be-boys grin. "Come on, buddy—during the war I was shacked up with a broad in a London flat, and we never stopped going at it, even when the apartment house took a direct hit."

The cop let out a half-grudging grunt of appreciation and said, "Awright—suit yourself, mister. I just wanted to warn you what you might be getting yourself into."

"Thanks," I said. "I'm dead on my feet and need to hit the rack. I probably won't be around that long."

But the cop was already wandering off, forgetting all about me.

So I sat in the room with the .45 in my lap and looked out the window, watching the reflections of nighttime Miami on the overcast sky, a small section of Miami Beach in the far background. Down on the street, the curious still milled and two construction trucks were pulling up to the curb to join the fire wagons. Across from the hotel, local TV mobile units had finished their pictures for the late news show and were packing away their gear.

I got up and went over to the bed and sat on its edge, put the .45 on the nightstand, picked up the phone, and dialed a number, and when a familiar voice answered, I said, "Hello, Bunny."

"Morgan?"

"That's right. You sound surprised to hear my voice."

Maybe she'd put out another *contract on her old friend....*

"How'd you get this number?"

"I got sharp eyes, kid. I read the dial on your phone on your desk."

Her voice was low and tremulous—for a cool customer, she was off her game.

"God, Morgan," she said, "I *heard* what happened."

"Who from?"

"It's all over the radio and TV."

"Ah."

She didn't say anything for a second, then: "I know what you must be thinking."

"Sure. You hate somebody long enough, given the opportunity, you'll kill him. It's a logical assumption."

"You can't *really* think I set you up...."

"Possibilities are possibilities, Bunny. It doesn't suit your style, but I'd still like to hear you say it."

She gave me that throaty laugh. "I'm glad you think me

still capable, big boy, but I'll say it. It wasn't me. Not even a little bit....that good enough for you?"

"Good enough, Bunny."

"That's all it takes? Just me saying it?"

"Why not? I can always tell if a broad is lying to me. I spent a lot of years honing this bullshit detector."

"What if I've perfected *my* technique," she said, something light in her tone now. "Maybe you *can't* tell."

"You're a broad, aren't you?"

"I was at my last physical."

"Then you're not lying. But if I were you, I'd try checking around the homestead. Look under a bed or two. Maybe you don't run as tight a ship over at the Club Mandor as you think."

"You're laying this on my doorstep?"

"I just figure maybe somebody has a big mouth over there. I don't like being made a patsy."

She sighed. "Way ahead of you, Morgan. I've already started things rolling. Where are you calling from?"

"Come on, Bunny," I said. "I'm not *that* confident in my bullshit detector."

I hung up without a goodbye, and went back to the window again, plopped in the comfortable chair, staring out of the darkness into the hazy lights of the city.

Somebody out there wants me dead, I thought. *Hell, maybe several somebodies.*

The bellboy who brought in the quartet of cold bottled beers folded the five spot into his pocket with a big grin. He seemed glad to have somebody to tell about all the excitement in the other wing. His accent said he was prob-ably not born here, but he spoke English just fine. Another Cuban, maybe.

On the face of it, the "accident" seemed simple enough—409 was a small suite with a kitchenette that contained a refrigerator, sink, and two-burner gas range. The last person who occupied it had been a middle-aged woman and her dog, five days ago. Assumption was, the maid who cleaned the place had accidentally turned on one of the jets, and the pilot light triggered the explosion.

I said, "Don't they check the rooms every day?"

The bellboy shrugged and shook his head. "This is not the Fontainebleau, *señor*. The room was clean, so why bother again, *si*?"

"Downstairs, I overheard somebody saying a guest was due to check into that room tonight."

"Yes, and he was a lucky person, that one."

"Sure as hell was." I popped open a bottle of beer and tasted it. "Things quieted down over there yet?"

"The hall, it is being cleaned up. I hear they will investi-gate more, tomorrow, the firemen and the police. But why do they bother?"

"What do you mean, kid?"

He shrugged. "This building is slowly and surely falling apart. One day they will have to close it entirely."

I nodded and tried the beer again. "I'd like to get over there and take a gander myself."

He frowned, shook his head. "No one is to go there, *señor*."

"For five bucks, I bet somebody could."

No frown now.

"For ten bucks, *señor*, I *know* somebody could."

The firefighters were long gone. The fire inspector had found more important things to inspect. A single ancient porter shoveling cracked plaster into a trash can was the sole occupant of the corridor. The guests had been transferred to other rooms on other floors, and temporary barricades had been set up at either end of the hall to keep the curious away.

That old Mexican guy with the broom and dustpan didn't even bother to look up when we arrived on the scene. When he had the trash can filled, he wheeled it away, as if cleaning up after exploding rooms was a common everyday occurrence around the Amherst.

Hell, maybe it was.

The split door to 409 hung on a loose hinge, still in position only because an L bend had diverted the force of the blast. Inside, nothing was left at all. Smoke still drifted, and water from fire hoses pooled like remnants of a bad indoor storm. The floor hadn't given way, but had been shattered, turned into an expanse of rubble; the ceiling had been ripped apart, exposing twisted, dry beams and only a hole remained where the outside wall had been, letting cool night in. Mattress stuffing was scattered around like moist confetti with barely recognizable fragments of what had been furniture.

Had a man been in there when the explosion occurred— me, for instance—all that would have been left of him would be colorful dabs of red to liven up the joint.

A small alcove had held the kitchen components, but was

relatively undamaged. The stove was there all right, an ancient thing whose knobs were so grease-laden, it took a hard twist to open them.

I let the small beam of a borrowed flashlight play around the remains a minute longer, then said, "The cops or firemen haul anything out of here?"

The bellboy gave me an odd glance. "*Si*. There was one who carried a small damaged box, very carefully. He and another talked for a long time before they left."

I nodded.

He studied me another moment, then said, "Tell me, *señor*, and I do not mean to pry, but...should this have been *your* room?"

"Why do you figure that?"

"Perhaps I have worked in the hotel business too long, for one my age. I sometimes think I see things that others, they miss."

"That can give a guy a leg up, I guess."

His nod was crisp, his grin a flash of white in a brown face. "It has been profitable on more than one occasion, *señor*."

The tone of his voice was a little pointed and I looked at him. "Maybe you'd like to make a profit out of that ability of yours right now."

"*Señor*, you have been most kind already. For the dollars you gave me, you have my eternal loyalty. Or for the rest of the night, at least."

I laughed. "And this includes your insights?"

Another nod. He whispered: "The old one, cleaning up outside?"

"Yeah?"

"A man in a fireman's hat, wearing a suit? I hear him tell the *viejo hombre* to report to him any visitors to this room. He gave the old one a card, a business card."

I flipped the flashlight off and handed it to him. I carefully stepped around the damp floor to the door and moved out into the corridor. The bellboy followed.

The hall was empty but for the ancient porter, back for another load, and his casual indifference to us was a lousy act. I walked up to him, flipped my wallet open then shut in front of his nose too fast for him to see what wasn't there; but to the old boy, it was a routine police gesture and he accepted it.

In my best official manner, I asked, "Anyone been around since our men left?"

He had one of those faces so grooved and wrinkled, you couldn't imagine what it once had looked like; his hair was wispy and white, the top of his skull a great big dead dandelion crown whose seeds weren't traveling.

He swallowed, didn't meet my eyes with his rheumy gaze, and shook his head. "No, *señor*. There has been nobody."

"Okay, pops—keep your eyes open. You know what to do."

"Yes, *senor*," he said, with as vigorous a nod as he could manage. "I have been instructed."

I walked down to the elevators, wondering if they'd add impersonating a cop to the other charges against me. The bellboy was tagging along, with a mischievous smile. We took the elevator to my floor and got off. The kid had been watching me, all the way.

Finally he said, "You are a strange one, *señor*. Or maybe all Americans are *loco*."

"I'm not nuts, *amigo*, just curious. A guy in a dull line of work like mine doesn't get to see excitement up close every day."

The smile stretched a little. "That would not be my description of you, *señor*."

"No?"

"No. You are very the much active man. Remember, I said there are things I do not miss?"

"Yeah. Sorry. Forgot the big rule for a second there."

"What rule is that, *señor*?"

"Don't shit a shitter."

He laughed. "Those are words of wisdom. It is always wise not to insult the intelligence of those around you. Even one in a menial position may provide the great insight, now and then."

"Damn, are you *all* college graduates around here?"

A white flash of smile again. "Not yet, *señor*…but I intend to be one day."

"*Amigo*," I told him, with a pat on the shoulder, "you'll make it all the way."

"I have the grades and the ambition. But the world turns on money, *señor*."

"Then maybe you'd like to add a little more to your piggy bank."

He looked at me with eyes narrowed and alert.

I said, "Somebody was in that room since it was cleaned after the last check-out. Somebody who left a package under the bed, with a timer on it. Luckily, like some bridegrooms on their wedding night, the thing went off prematurely."

His eyes widened. "But it has been five days since the last guest..."

"This would have been recent—in the last day or so. Before then, nobody knew *who* was going to occupy that room."

His voice was very soft. "I see...."

"You can't be the only one around here who notices things. Someone else on the hotel staff must have seen him. Or anyway there's a hell of a chance of that."

Nodding, the boy said, "I understand, *señor*."

"Be discreet, son."

He grinned. "That is the way of the world at *any* hotel."

After he took the elevator down, I walked back to my room and stretched out on the bed.

A couple of things were pretty obvious.

Luis Saldar's operation had one big goddamn leak in it. So far seven adults were in on the hardcore facts of this particular junket and if one or more of them hadn't tried to tap me out directly, they could have tipped somebody else to it...either by accident or design.

The other obvious factor was this: somebody wanted me dead bad enough to put a hurry-up job like this botched hotel room bombing in motion—meaning there would be another try. Maybe with more care, next time.

Or maybe not.

Either way, all I had to do now was make myself available for next time, and be ready for it.

Well, here I was.

I fell asleep thinking, jarred from sleep twice because some odd little piece about Jaimie Halaquez and his seventy-five-thousand-buck haul kept rattling around loose; then finally I fell into a fitful doze…

…until an insistent tapping jolted me awake, and I sat up with the .45 in my hand.

When I reached the door, I yanked it open and the bellboy was staring down the hole in the muzzle of the gun with a shocked expression, a real *ay caramba* moment, though he didn't say it.

Then I yanked him inside, eased the door shut, and shoved the rod in my belt.

"Sorry, *amigo*," I said.

He nodded, feeling for his voice. "Looking down that gun barrel, *señor*, is a most uncomfortable feeling." Little beads of sweat had popped out on his forehead.

"No shit." I checked my watch. In another half-hour the sun would be up. "It's getting late, my friend. Or early. Not quite sure which."

"Either way, there is still time."

"For what?"

He licked his lips nervously and patted his forehead dry with his sleeve. "The old one, the porter you spoke to?"

"Yeah?"

Slowly, his eyes crawled up my face until they were meeting my own. "He is in a closet near where the explosion happened. He is quite dead, *señor*. Someone has broken his neck for him…very expertly, I would say."

I said, "Damn," very softly.

"His body, it is cold and...and stiff. I do not know much about such things, but I know enough to say it must have happened some time ago. Perhaps shortly after you talked to him in the hallway."

"You haven't reported this?"

"Just to you, *señor*."

"If you hadn't found the body, who would be most likely to discover it?"

He didn't have to think about it. "In the morning, the maid whose equipment is in that closet, she would find him, maybe. Or perhaps the police, when they come back to investigate more in that blown-up room. That is why there is still time for you to leave, *señor*."

"How did *you* come across the dead guy?"

"I was trying to find out things for you. I went to his room first and he was not there. The old one never goes out at night. I had hoped to speak to him. He is like a ghost, that one. He could watch, he could spy, and no one would notice —an old man in a menial position, he is invisible. Until his death, at least."

"What do you mean, kid?"

"Whoever put him in the closet failed to close the door tight. I went back to the hallway, where we were earlier, where the explosion room is? Looking for the old man. I notice that door, it is...what is the word...*ajar* So I open it, only to close it better, harder, and then...there he was."

I waited a second, watching him close. "And you haven't spoken to *anyone* about this?"

"*Señor!*" His tone was sharp, his eyes wide. "The maid, let *her* do the discovering. I know nothing of this, should anyone ask…but it is important that *you* know."

I gave him a smile and squeezed his arm. "Thanks, *amigo*."

"What does it mean, *señor*, this death? This…murder?"

I shrugged. "Probably that the old boy was paid to plant the gimmick. Maybe that's why the timing was off. He didn't know enough about setting the mechanism, and it blew early."

"But to *kill* him…why? Surely he would never talk to the police, and risk arrest for himself."

"Nobody was worried about him going to the cops. Whoever set this in motion, they know I'm still alive…and were afraid *I'd* get to him."

"*Señor*…you must go. Before the body is found."

I fished out the roll of bills Saladar had given me and peeled off a hundred-dollar leaf.

"Enroll in some courses on me, *amigo*," I said.

"This is not necessary." His eyes were glittering. "But I am very grateful."

"Back at you, kid."

He thanked me again and slipped the C-note in his pocket.

I glanced at the roll of bills again, found a ten, and handed it to him with a grin. "And check me out, would you? I like to keep my bills paid up."

The parents of Magruder Harris had optimistically over-named their offspring.

Magruder had grown up to become a bail bondsman who was never known by anything except Muddy. Whether

Muddy's folks were proud of him, or alive or dead, I had no idea. What I did know was, the beach house and the matching set of Caddies he owned, a convertible and hardtop, hadn't come out of the interest he charged on his bonds.

To the right people, Muddy was known as a fixer and information source par excellence. His eyes and ears—and that filing cabinet mind of his—had cornered a unique market on contacts, and if the price was right, what you needed to know would be for sale.

Heavyset but not fat, well dressed but not flashy, with fleshy features and a comb-over that wasn't fooling anybody, Muddy sat behind a battered mahogany desk, feet propped on top, his cloudy blue eyes peering at me around the thin tendril of smoke from the butt that swung from his lips.

I said, "Long time, Muddy."

He barely nodded. "Morgan." The cigarette shifted to a corner of his mouth seemingly of its own volition. "Wondered when you'd be around."

"News travels fast."

"Always has and always will," Muddy shrugged, and took a drag on the cigarette.

My watch said it was a little after nine. Outside the night had tucked the city under its blanket. I'd spent the day holed up, sleeping, eating, and making phone calls, all in a room at a hotel picked out by nobody but me. I asked him, "Working late?"

"Nope. Just sitting here expecting you."

"Why?"

"You called Kirk in New York, he called me, so I waited."

He paused a second, then added, "It *has* been a while, Morgan."

"Uh-huh."

"Long time between scores."

"I've been busy."

"I'll say." The cigarette was almost down to his lips, so he plucked it out, pinched it, and tossed the stub in a wastebasket. "Kirk was plenty happy to hand you over to me. Right now you're too hot for anybody."

"So, then, I shouldn't let the door hit me on the ass on the way out?"

"Naw, hell, man. Make yourself at home." He folded his hands behind his head and leaned back, those cloudy eyes watching me with interest. "That was supposed to have been you in the Amherst Hotel, wasn't it?"

I pulled a chair out from the wall with my foot and slid into it. "That's right."

For the first time since I got there, Muddy Harris grinned. "The boys in blue were pretty sore last night."

"Really? Is this where I bust out crying?"

"Homer Carey had you pegged as familiar but didn't hit the mug books fast enough to make you. You damn near blew it, though, sticking around that dump that long. Did you know the locals got a murder warrant out on you?"

"I read the papers this morning. All it said was an old low-level hotel employee got himself killed by person or persons unknown."

Muddy grunted. "I guess they aren't passing everything out to the press...or else maybe the newshounds are cooperating by keeping it quiet a little while longer." An eyebrow raised above a smoky blue eye. "Your name still moves mountains, though. A lot of strange faces are popping up these days, and they're all carrying badges."

"Good for them."

Muddy squinted at me. "You knock off the old Mexie, Morgan?"

"You know that's not my style, buddy."

"Didn't think it was. If I did, we wouldn't be here talking."

"Even so, Mud, you're taking a big chance right now."

"Life is all chances, Morgan. If you don't take a chance, you don't win a prize. Like, I coulda had the cops waiting right here with me, and picked up that gravy they got ready for whoever turns you in. Trouble is, I don't get to spend it, because some punk figures me for a squealer and picks me off, or some friend of yours decides to do an unasked-for favor and squeezes my neck for me."

He shrugged rather grandly.

"This way it's better," he said. "Some way, shape, or form, I'll come out of this thing with a little more bread than when I went in. Playing the angles, but not crossing anybody who's my friend…or who's too dangerous *not* to be my friend. Follow?"

"I'm in the business, too, remember?"

"Yeah, but how does it feel to be hunted?"

"Keeps me on my toes. My chances of survival go up, thanks to all this experience I'm getting."

"That, Morgan, is one hell of an attitude, even for you. Like that cop…what's his name? Oh yeah, Walter Crowley.

Like Crowley said, whoever takes you down gets the brass ring."

"Screw Walter Crowley."

A faint grin cracked Muddy's lips. "I think you already did—or screwed him over, anyway. He had you and now he doesn't. That's why he's so damn mad. Taking it so damn personal."

"Is it."

"By the way, Morg—he's got it figured out, you know."

"What has he got figured out?"

"How you busted out of that net they had around you."

"Oh?"

"They got a partial description of a guy wearing coveralls from Farango's Car Wash, but nobody that size works there. The cop had a pretty good look at the girl, though. Especially at her titties. They're shaking down the area looking for her."

"They better be pretty good at breaking alibis, if they find her."

Another shrug, not so grand. "Just thought I'd mention it. Now, my old *compadre*, what can I do for you?"

"You can run a check on the old man killed at that hotel. Somebody paid him off to plant that charge in the room."

His smile was just another fold in the fleshy face. "That's what I thought you'd ask for."

"Can do?"

"Maybe. How much do you think he got for the gig?"

"Not big money. Well, maybe big for him."

"Chump change to take out Morgan the Raider? How far fall the mighty."

I waved that off. "My name wouldn't have meant jack to him, so the price would've had to be high enough for him to take it on, but not enough to make him suspicious."

"You mean not suspicious enough for a possible blackmail shot later on."

"Right." This time I shrugged. "I'd guess five hundred bottom, a grand tops. It would be cash, and small bills. Chances are the old man didn't have a chance to spend it, and he sure wouldn't carry it around on him. He was a loner, according to my inside source. So anybody making contact with the old boy might get noticed."

Muddy squinted at me. "You got it pretty well figured out yourself."

"All part of a pattern, Mud, my man. Human nature doesn't vary that much."

"Okay, I'll look into it." He leaned forward to light himself a new smoke. "Anything else?"

"Yeah. What do you know about the Consummata?"

Muddy's eyes got less cloudy. "Not my scene, Morg."

"What do you know, Muddy?"

He shook his head in a "no way" fashion. "That world's dark and dank and dangerous, my friend. If she even exists at all. They say she's done business in every major city here and overseas. That she can give you girls you can whip and screw and even kill if you want. Whatever your perverted pleasure, whatever your sicko taste might desire."

I made an appreciative face. "Well, she accomplishes a hell of a lot, for somebody who maybe doesn't exist. Is she in town?"

He got coy; it didn't become him. "I don't know. I haven't heard."

"But you'll ask?"

"I'd rather not, Morgan."

"But you will." I tossed a couple of bills on the desktop. "That's a retainer. Enough?"

His sigh was long-suffering. "I guess it'll do for a start. I suppose I don't contact you."

"That's right."

"I'm in the book," Muddy told me.

I was just going out when he said, "Morgan!"

I turned. "Yeah?"

"You already got enough problems, with Crowley and that federal bunch. This Consummata dame, that whole whips-and-chains crowd, and the freaks who dig that crazy pain scene? I'd advise against going anywhere near it or her."

"You would, huh? Why?"

Muddy's smile was a nasty thing lurking in the folds of flesh. "Oh, don't know, Morg. Maybe 'cause you might get a spanking."

CHAPTER SIX

At ten-forty, I tucked into a phone booth alongside a gas station and dialed the office number of the Mandor Club, but the line was busy.

I had a cup of coffee at the diner across the street, used their payphone for my second try—another busy signal. A slice of Key Lime pie later, I headed back across the street to the gas station booth, and this time I got Bunny.

Not wanting to chance a phone tap, I let her identify me by voice, then—before she could say anything but hello—said, "The truck with the shipment of cutlery you ordered just came in. I know it's late, ma'am, but you said call when it arrived. You ready to take delivery?"

Her hesitation was just right—a businesswoman thinking, not a conspirator covering. "Yeah, Jonesy—you might as well bring the stuff on over. Wait, on second thought, send it over to my apartment at the Hillside. Have your guy give the package to the doorman. He'll sign for it."

"Sure thing, ma'am," I said, and hung up.

In its day, the Hillside had been one of the better apartment buildings, one of those pink stucco *art moderne* jobs that looked so spiffy in the thirties, but now were faded, pockmarked and crumbly. A few face-lifts hadn't helped much, and now the Hillside just stood there among others of its ilk like aging old broads gathered to talk about what used to be and what might have been.

From my spot in the shadows, I could cover both ends of the street, a boring wait because anybody who lived here was already in bed, and most of the cars cruising through were taxis going back to their stands. The .45 was in a shoulder rig now—not a great one, but passable, considering it had come from a pawn shop. Anyway, the rod felt nice and snug under my arm, and was far less conspicuous than just being shoved in my waistband.

At twenty after twelve, a white Ford station wagon rounded the corner, and turned in just past the entrance of the Hillside, into a small side lot, and found an open stall.

Moments later, I heard the car door slam, but wasn't sure it was Bunny till she came around and paused under a streetlight. She might have been a veteran streetwalker if her white fur coat and blue velour pantsuit hadn't put her in a whole other class. She was getting keys out of a purse, but not for the front door of the place—there was a uni-formed doorman just inside who tipped his hat and opened one of the two glass doors for her. The entryway was well lighted and I could easily make out Bunny's activities within.

The gal knew the ropes, all right. She took her time looking in her mailbox, sorting out a few envelopes, reading a letter, giving anybody who might have been following her a chance to show themselves, not so much to her as to me.

I waited maybe three minutes, then left my shadows and walked across. You'd never know her eyes had left the letter she was reading—or pretending to read—as she stood there in the foyer in no hurry at all.

But I knew she had spotted me crossing the street when she approached the doorman, granted him a lovely smile, and said something to him, gesturing behind her as she did.

Then the doorman nodded, tipped his hat to her, and disappeared into a room across the mini-lobby marked STORAGE just as I was approaching the front doors. She quickly let me in, whispered "Two A, one floor up," and I left her in the foyer to deal with the doorman and the fool's errand she'd sent him on.

I took the stairs and waited at the top of the landing. I could hear some muffled conversation between her and the doorman below, then maybe thirty seconds later, she emerged from the self-service elevator down the hall.

Bunny was a good-looking broad for her age—what, forty-five? Fifty? One of those larger-than-life dames, the sort that went out with Mae West, Jean Harlow, and Jane Russell. She'd held up well, had all her curves and no apparent flab; whether she exercised or just drew decent genes, I had no idea. But she was the kind of older woman who could give a guy lessons, purple-streaked blonde bouffant and all.

I let her open the door, stepped inside while she closed it and flipped on the light switch. She started to say something, but I tapped my mouth with one forefinger and my ear with the other.

She returned the nod, motioning me to tag along.

Taking time out only to hang up her white fur coat in the front closet, she gave the apartment a professional systematic search, starting with the windows onto the street.

The pad was small, considering how important and wealthy a woman Bunny was, just a living room, bedroom, small kitchen, and bath; but she probably had other residences. This was one appointed in white with sleek, rounded, off-white furnishings that fit the *art moderne* look of the old building, though the carpet was a more current pink shag.

We wound up back in the living room.

"No bugs," she said. "You're sure a suspicious bastard."

"I'm alive, aren't I? How secure is your office?"

"I have it swept once a month," she said, "and I don't mean the rugs. The law can't legally tap the phones, but it gets done anyway, and I'm not exactly in a business where I could lodge a complaint."

"Understood. Guess the phone game I played was unnecessary."

"No, with what's been going on, there's no sense taking chances. Now sit down and take a load off. Want a drink?"

I plopped onto a plump couch that proved as comfy as it looked. "Got a cold beer handy?"

"Coming right up."

She hip-swayed out to the kitchen—no come-on, just the kind of natural gait that's made the world go round since Eve was a rib.

I heard her pop a pair of cans in there, and she came back in, sat beside me and passed me a very cold Schlitz.

"That's some smart cookie," she said, "they got heading up the outfit that almost busted your ass."

"Walter Crowley."

"That's the one."

"Well, he wasn't smart enough to hold onto me the first time around." I sipped icy beer. Nectar of the gods. "Bastard may have had a lead that'll take him to Gaita."

Bunny studied me over the top of her beer can. "You do get around," she told me.

"Think so?"

She nodded. "I heard the same thing. So we covered for her. Rounded up a trustworthy lookalike who filled in for her, and a good-size Cuban who could make it stick by admitting he was the guy caught rolling around in the dark with her."

"One of my fellow employees at the Farango Car Wash?"

"No, but the big, not-so-dumb galoot works for the laundry that handles the Farango account. He told the cops—local and federal alike—that he wore those coveralls home, to put on while working on his car."

"Put on is right." I chuckled appreciatively. "Not a bad story."

"Not bad at all. It all tied in. The cop even identified them, much to Crowley's disgust and dismay."

"Nice. Thanks."

She laughed.

"What?" I asked.

"The cop? The one who identified our lookalike gal as Gaita? When he first saw our substitute, he asked if he could see her with her top down. Thought he might be able to identify her better."

I almost snorted beer through my nose, laughing. "Guess you can't blame a guy for trying."

Her laughter subsided. "I just wish that's all there was to

it. I don't like having a leak in this operation, and we've obviously sprung one. Think it came from someone on this end?"

"I hate to say it, doll, but I'm inclined to think so. I doubt it came from Luis Saladar's side. I mean, this all went down too quickly. How far can you trust the girls at your place?"

Bunny took a slow sip of the beer and shrugged. "Who knows? How far you can you trust any girl on the game? I treat them good, better than good, and I don't take on anybody who seems hinky to me...but every girl in that line of trade is damaged goods, Morg."

"I know. It's an old, sad, and very true story."

She nodded. "Every one has something to hide, or something that might break them. They're scared, most of them, or they wouldn't be there in the first place. If Daddy wasn't their first sexual experience, their uncle was, or some neighbor or school bully."

"Yet I've known girls on the game who liked their work."

"Some do. Some actually enjoy it, at least part of the time. But they all have come to a place in their lives where this is their best option for making for a living...and almost all of them are scared."

"Who else knew that you were helping me? Who else could know about us taking Jaimie Halaquez on?"

Her frown made her years show, wrinkles coming out from hiding. "Nobody that I know of. Just Gaita and Tami, but then, *some* of the others *had* to sense something was up...and might have put the pieces together." Her dark blues locked onto me. "What are you thinking, Morgan? I can see the wheels turning."

I shrugged. "Just that Jaimie Halaquez was a regular patron

of yours, Bunny. Sometimes girls on the game have special clients—sometimes they even marry them. Maybe one of your girls latched on to the son of a bitch."

"Fuck," she said, that single dirty word at odds with her quiet elegance, even if she was a whorehouse madam. "You were right the first time—Halaquez is a son of a bitch. He wasn't exactly well liked, Morgan. The guy was a bastard, a real louse."

"Still...girls have been known to fall for real louses." I grinned at her. "I've even had a few fall for me."

She didn't grin back. "Not a louse like this one. He paid women to humiliate him, and then he took it out on them."

"I heard that before. Maybe you could be more specific."

She swallowed, seeming ill at ease—and Bunny was *not* the ill-at-ease type. "Morgan, Halaquez would want that... that sick submissive shit, whole nine yards. Handcuffs, chains, whips, ball gags—you know?"

"I know. Not my scene, but I know."

"But *after*? After, he would beat the girl, like I told you. But on several occasions he...I *know* they're prostitutes, Morgan, I have no illusion what I am or what they are...but he raped them. He goddamn *raped them*, Morgan."

Nausea fought the beer in my stomach. "And how does a whore go to the cops with that complaint?"

Bunny's tone was icy. "She doesn't. She doesn't." She shuddered. "He could really rip a girl up, that bastard."

"Which girl?"

"Well, he had a few favorites, but not many of my girls would put up with him, after the first time."

I put a hand on her shoulder. "Keep it in mind, Bunny.

Someone's holding hands with a killer, and that someone could be the next one taken out of the game."

She shook her head, and a purple tendril fought its way free from the bouffant. "What girl in her right mind would want to be with a sick sadistic rapist like Halaquez?"

"Maybe a girl whose first experience was having Daddy rape her. Maybe a girl who likes money. Don't ask me, Bunny —find a shrink, or write Dear Abby. But it's possible. Did you put the word out about that Consummata dame?"

She made a dismissive gesture. "I placed a few calls. Nothing. It must just be a rumor."

"Make *more* calls. If this woman is the queen of sado-masochism, like you and others in the know keep telling me, she's right up Halaquez's dirty alley."

Bunny shot me an angry look and slammed the beer can on the glass coffee table nearby. "Damn it, Morgan! Since you showed up, there's been nothing but trouble."

"Hell, don't look at me. I didn't ask for it."

"Maybe so, but it seems to grow where you go, like a sickness you're carrying. Typhoid Morgan, that's you!"

"Thanks a bunch."

She sighed. Shook her head. "Take today. *Today*, I had to go down to the morgue and identify a body, and—"

I sat up. "*Whose* body?"

She tried waving it off. "Just a guy. Former client."

"Just a guy? So why did the cops call *you* to make the I.D.?"

"He had an address book on him—six names in it, five untraceable, the other is lucky me. He's been coming into the Mandor Club off and on for maybe three years. No trouble, just a customer the kids liked, and who wasn't afraid to spend money. We knew him as Richard Best. Dick Best." She laughed a little. "Some of the girls called him the Best Dick."

"Why, was he hung like a horse?"

"Almost the opposite. He came to the Mandor to be pampered, and half the time, he never got around to the sex. He was no spring chicken—maybe sixty, sixty-five? He was looking for company, for pleasant female companionship. An ideal client for my girls, the polar opposite of Jaimie Halaquez."

"What did he look like?"

"Oh, he was nothing special. Just a medium guy, medium height, average looking."

"Hair color?"

"Brown."

"Eye color?"

"Brown. He kind of reminded me of that old actor, William Powell? But not quite as handsome. Nice man, though. Real sweetheart."

"How well did you know him, Bunny?"

She thought back, and her expression conveyed a fondness for her subject. "Well enough, I guess. We talked plenty of times. We'd sit in the bar and talk old times."

"Why, had he known you before?"

"Well, if so, I didn't remember him. But he remembered me and my husband, the old fox, from the days when we were in the papers regularly." Her chin lifted, her eyes rolled back in remembering. "Used to tell me how much he admired my husband, and how he thought my better half had gotten framed into prison. *Framed?* Hell, the old fox worked good and damn hard to get behind bars. He deserved everything he got!"

"You're preaching to the choir, Bunny,"

Her eyes were distant. "…not that I didn't love the slick ol' bastard, though."

Time to get her back on track. "What was it that turned Richard Best into a corpse?"

"Broken neck. He got slugged with something. His cash, watch and ring were gone, and his place turned inside out. He lived in an apartment, nothing fancy. Lived there and died there."

"Still, he must have had enough worth killing for."

Bunny kicked her shoes off and put her feet up on the coffee table. "Morgan, anybody who has anything is worth killing for these days. That area where he lived—two robberies and a mugging in the past three months. Damn. World's losing its moral compass, don't you think?"

All whorehouse madams were philosophers.

I asked, "Ever have a regular patron turn up dead before, Bunny?"

She gave me sideways look laced with a tight smile. "Come on, Morgan. Anybody who makes a whorehouse a regular stop is *some* kind of target for *somebody*. I've seen familiar faces in the news one day and the obits the next." Again she shuddered, and sipped beer. "It's just that I don't like to get called in to identify bodies."

That tight little feeling was running up my spine again. I could sense it running across my shoulders and bunching up into my neck.

"I don't like it, Bunny. With what we've been up to, having a stiff turn up for you to identify?…I don't like it at all."

"You think *I* do?"

I leaned back in the softness of the couch; it tried to soothe me, but it didn't work. "Think you can find anything else out about this particular corpse—Richard Best?"

"Like how?" she asked suspiciously.

"Surely you have friends on the department."

"Me and the fuzz don't exactly socialize."

"I didn't ask if you socialized with them. You're friendly with somebody or you wouldn't be open for business. Somebody picks up a monthly envelope of green stuff. Or is it weekly?"

She reached for a package of Virginia Slims on the coffee table, selected one, lighted it up with a silver decorative lighter, and blew the smoke at the ceiling.

Reluctantly, she said, "Okay…so I know a few people."

I gestured with an open hand. "You could show a sign of interest in the dead guy. I mean, they already know he was a client, so you go around and say ol' Dick Best was a good, even beloved patron of the Mandey arts, much missed by all the girls. Then offer up a cheap burial if nobody claims the body."

She smirked in quiet disgust. "Yeah? Then what?"

"Make a simple inquiry. I'd like to know what the autopsy report shows."

"Damn it, Morgan! You…"

"Yes or no?"

Something in my voice stopped her, made her look at me closely a few seconds, then she said, "Okay, I've been a chump before." She dragged on the cigarette again. Shook her head. "I don't know why the hell I'm doing this."

"I do," I said.

"Really?"

"Sure. You're a nosy old broad."

This time her grin was quick and open. She looked me up and down with a friendly, salacious gaze. "I'm not *that* old, Morgan. I think I could still teach you a thing or two."

"If I had the time, doll, I wouldn't mind learning."

Her forehead crinkled. "Time? Where the hell are you off to *now*?"

I got to my feet. "Why, a whorehouse, Bunny. Not just any whorehouse, either—an elegant place called the Mandor Club with a secret back entrance into a lovely doll's private boudoir."

"Gaita doesn't come cheap," she said. "Takes real dough to buy a night with her."

I gave her my biggest grin. "Hell, kid—she offered it to me free the last time."

She blinked at me in astonishment. "And, what? You're going back for seconds?"

"Naw. I turned her down. I'm saving myself for you."

She was still laughing when I closed the door on her.

I didn't bother with the elevator. I took the stairs and paused at the bend by the landing. One corner of the building partially obscured the entryway, and if the doorman was standing in his area, I sure couldn't see him.

At this hour, with nothing much to do, there was a good chance our man in uniform was sacked out somewhere, and

I was ready to make an unhurried exit when I got that funny feeling up my back again, and held still.

The foyer was a mini-lobby that had been laid out like a blunt T, with a stairwell to either wing going up from the end of the arms, the self-service elevator in the middle facing the entry doors. When I had come in, the doorman had been sent to the storage closet at the other end, and at that time the overhead lights had been on. Now only my end was illuminated, and the other side was too deep in shadow to tell if anyone was there.

Somebody had a trap all set and waiting.

Very slowly, I edged back up the stairs to the next floor, walked the length of the corridor to the other wing, and went down the metal-and-tile stairs without making any sound at all. I snaked the .45 out, balanced it in my hand, held it under my arm to thumb the hammer back so no *click* would be audible, then crouched down in the shadows and stepped around the bend.

He was there, all right, his back partially toward me, a dark silhouette with a long-barreled, silencer-tipped gun dangling from his hand. I only stood there a second, knowing he hadn't heard me, but when I saw a tiny involuntary twitch, I knew he had felt me there like an animal would, and I took two quick steps forward as he spun, and I kicked the gun out of his hand.

The weapon made a metallic clunk on the floor, but didn't discharge, as its owner reacted like a cat, flipping sideways in a roll, a sharp hiss spitting between his teeth. He either didn't see the gun in my hand or didn't expect me to have one, because his hand whipped inside his coat, came out with a blade and he uncoiled from the floor like a spring in a lunge toward my chest and I laid the .45 across his ear as I sidestepped and he twisted and went down with a funny whistling sound and lay there jerking a few times before he made a soft sigh and went limp.

I waited a moment, then flipped him over with my foot.

The knife meant for me was hilt-deep in his chest, his fingers still gripped in a deathlock around the handle.

It only took a second to locate the doorman.

He was huddled in the storage closet, an ugly red and blue welt across his forehead. He was alive, but unconscious, and was going to stay that way a few hours. He was in no particular need of first aid and I didn't give him any.

Instead, I went back out into the foyer, listened intently, while the quiet hung over the place like a blanket. The whole thing had been almost noiseless anyway.

I checked the dead man.

There was no wallet on him and his clothes were non-descript enough to make label identification impossible. He had sixty dollars in bills in a side pocket, but had been professional enough not to carry change, keys or anything else that might rattle. I put him in his middle forties, but from his features I couldn't tag his national origin. He had enough of a tan to have been in the area a while, and the one hand that still clutched the hilt of the knife was soft enough to indicate he didn't do any manual labor. He might have been Latin, but I couldn't be sure.

I'd thought this might be Halaquez himself, and was relieved it wasn't—I wouldn't have minded that evil bastard being dead, of course, but I really did hope to find the money he'd stolen from my Cuban friends first.

Whoever he was, I added his bills to my own roll, found the gun I had kicked out of his hand and looked at it in the light. It was a Spanish-made job in beautiful shape except for where the serial numbers had been filed off. I stuck it in my belt, stood up and listened again. Still quiet.

From the call board in the foyer, I pushed in Bunny's number, told her to get down in a hurry with her car keys and to take the stairs, and went back into the shadows and waited, hoping the apartment building didn't have any late arrivals.

When she got there, she was out of breath, and I cracked open the storage closet door enough for the light to bathe the body on the floor nearby.

She saw the doorman and the dead guy at the same time, turned wide eyes on me and whispered softly, "Your handiwork, Morgan?"

"Just this one." I nudged the corpse with my toe. "You know him? Maybe it's another dead patron you can identify."

"Morgan...."

"Take a good close look, doll."

She didn't like it, yet she did it. She would have pulled away almost at once, but something stopped her and she looked again.

When she stood up, she was frowning. "I *have* seen him, I think."

"Mandor patron?"

Bunny shook her head. "No, if that were the case, I really would be able to make an I.D. With this one, I can't be sure."

Deliberately, drawing in breath as if it were courage, she bent down, studied the dead features carefully, then pulled herself up.

"Morg, I'm not positive, but I think he used to do something for Jaimie Halaquez. A driver, maybe. General gofer." The broader implication of that got to her then, and her hand went to her mouth. "But...why *here*, Morgan? Where I *live*?"

"Somebody's worked out the connection between you and me. They figured I might make a contact with you, after the business at the hotel, to see if there was a leak at your place of business. In other words, we both did exactly as was expected of us. And somebody, probably Halaquez, set a trap."

Her eyes were wild. "But...*nobody* knew I was going to see you tonight. We were careful on the phone, I checked for bugs, what the hell could—"

I gave her half a grin. "Honey, all they had to do was wait and watch until I showed up. The logical place to contact you would be here. If I'd shown up at the club, somebody would have tipped them from there."

"Who, Morgan?"

"I don't know...but I'll sure as hell find out."

Bunny shook her head, obviously rattled. "What about..." She pointed at the dead guy on the floor. "...*him*?"

"I'll take care of that. There's no phone down here, so he probably didn't tip anybody about my presence. As far as the world is concerned, doll, this was just a burglary attempt that went nowhere. So the doorman got himself slugged."

"His name is George. He's a very nice man."

"Swell. Pay him enough to keep his mouth shut, would you? To limit your exposure with the cops on this thing?"

"*Somebody* will find George, and…"

"*You'll* find George, Bunny," I said, taking her by the shoulders, firmly. "Georgie Porgie's going to sleep until morning, and your excuse for finding him is…are you getting this?"

"Yes. Yes."

"Your excuse is that you were checking on a package that was supposed to be delivered here. You faked him out with that story tonight, right?"

"Right…."

"So he'll probably buy it, and let it go like that. Particularly if there's a nice tip involved. Besides, attempted break-ins around here aren't all that unusual. Now, let's have your car keys. I need to borrow your wheels."

This was all moving a little fast for her. "Well, okay…."

"Tomorrow I'll tell you where to pick your buggy up. Cool?"

But she didn't say, "Cool." She just handed over the keys silently, watched me a moment, then said, "It's more than just Jaimie Halaquez, isn't it, Morgan?"

She was right, but she didn't need to know that.

So I just shrugged and said, "I don't know what the hell else it could be."

"It could be that forty million bucks they say you hijacked."

"Is that all you girls think about?" I asked. "Money?"

I reached out, gave a half-turn to the bulb in the wall bracket that had been unscrewed and let light flood the area.

The dead guy seemed to look up at me, eyes half open. The knife was in so hard, there was no blood showing around the wound at all. He looked a little silly like that. Death can be so goddamned undignified. The saving grace is, when you're dead, you don't really give much of a shit.

I heard Bunny suck her breath in, then she turned toward the stairway.

I called out to her: "Two things!"

She looked back at me like she was risking getting turned into a pillar of salt. "Yes?"

"I want you to call our mutual friend Pedro over in Little Havana for me, and give him a message."

She listened, then nodded and said, "What's the other thing?"

"Bring me down an old sheet, would you? I have to wrap this boy up. Might not be necessary if you didn't drive a station wagon, but I don't have a trunk to stuff him in, so...."

She shivered as she nodded, then ran up the stairs, came back quickly with a sheet, and without a word ran back up again.

Leaving me to do what I had to do.

CHAPTER SEVEN

They say criminals return to the scene of the crime, if for no other reason than to check for evidence left in the sloppy heat of the moment.

But there's another reason, too—sometimes the scene of the crime is the one place nobody thinks to look for you.

Little Havana wasn't the scene of any crime of mine, not exactly; but nobody figures you'll go back to somewhere you fled. The sprawling neighborhood just west of downtown stretched west from the Miami River for a mile or more. Near midnight, bustling Calle Ocho—Eighth Street, the area between Seventeenth and Twenty-seventh Avenues— lacked some of its robust flavor, though enough coffee shops and cigar stores remained open after midnight for their pungent aromas to add even more spice to the rhythmic sounds of Latin music pulsing behind barroom windows.

The block where I wound up wasn't lively, not right now, no packs of *muchachos* on the loose, to help or hinder, the restaurants and other mom-and-pop shops closed. Still, I only had to knock once at the doorway next to the *bodega* before I got service—Pedro Navarro was right there, waiting.

If he'd been sleeping when Bunny called to tell him I was coming, he was wide awake and alert now, still just a funny little guy with a *bandito* mustache. He looked stiff and proper in his pale yellow pleated button-down shirt and loose tan trousers and leather sandals, his smile forced as it fought back worry.

Soon we were all at the kitchen table in the Navarro living quarters above the grocery store, sharing small cups of hot black Cuban coffee—Pedro, his wife Maria, and Luis Saladar —the latter summoned by the man of the house, at my request.

They sat across the table from me, their faces drawn in concentration, the nervous movement of their hands the only evidence of their fear.

I'd already filled them in about the now-deceased visitor who'd come looking for me at Bunny's apartment house.

Pedro said, "*Señor* Morgan, what of the…the remains of this *asesino*? Do you require help in his…*its*…disposal?"

I waved that off. "Naw, buddy, but thanks. I dumped him in Domino Park on my way here."

All of their eyes widened, even those of Saladar, who had been around such things.

"Don't worry, *amigos*," I said, and sipped at the little cup. Strong as it was hot. "That stretch of street was deserted, and the park wasn't exactly busy—no old men playing checkers this time of night."

They didn't seem to know what to say.

Finally Saladar managed, "But why would such a person search you out, *Señor* Morgan?"

"Well, it's not the militia. They'd just as soon catch me breathing." I sipped more coffee. "Bunny thinks the dead guy worked for Halaquez."

Maria, alarm in both her voice and eyes, said, "How could Halaquez *know* where you would be?"

"Good question."

Pedro said, "If somehow he did know, he is very capable of sending a man to remove you, *señor*. Halaquez might be afraid that you would find him, and—"

"Maybe," I said, cutting off my host. I watched his face closely. "But why send somebody before I've even begun the hunt? After all, you people didn't hire me to *kill* this clown. It's a straight retrieval job."

Pedro squinted in thought. "I do not follow, *señor*...."

"Seventy-five thousand bucks," I said, "is real money, I'll grant you. But it doesn't justify sending an assassin to take me out."

"Perhaps not, *señor*," Saladar said. "But if one considers the *reputation* of Morgan the Raider, it might well seem *prudent*."

"Doubtful." I let a few seconds of silence sink in, then added, "Could it be something else? Could it be more than the money?"

In turn, they looked at each other, their puzzlement palpable.

Pedro said, "I am sorry, *Señor* Morgan, but I do not understand."

"Never mind." I grunted. "Tell me about Gaita."

Mildly defensive, Pedro said, "We trust her with our lives, *señor*."

"That's your choice. But trusting her with *mine* is my call. I want chapter and verse."

"*Señor?*"

"I want the whole damn dossier."

This also confused Pedro, but Luis Saladar knew exactly what I meant.

The trimly bearded man leaned back in his chair—again he wore a dignified white suit with a bolo tie—and his eyes focused on me steadily, rarely blinking as he spoke.

"My friend, this young woman's parents were killed by Castro's men before her eyes. With the bodies of her mother and papa nearby, several of these soldiers...they had their way with her."

"They raped her."

"They raped her, *señor*, yes. She was but a child of twelve or perhaps thirteen, you understand...yet what they did to her, she understood, and she learned at this age how to hate— how to hate very well."

"Makes sense."

"She came to this country aboard a small boat with six others. Two died of malnourishment before finally the Coast Guard towed them ashore. She was an independent child... true, she made her living by becoming a..."

He couldn't make himself say it, and found other words.

"...by *catering* to the needs of men. But like all of us, she deals with whatever commodity she has available. And her work for the cause, it has been exemplary."

I nodded. "*Novios?*"

But it was Maria who took the liberty of answering: "No sweethearts, *Señor* Morgan. No boys, no men. Since Gaita's experience at the hands of Castro's pigs that awful night, so many years ago? She has little to do with the male sex."

"Unless she's charging a male *for* sex, you mean?"

She took no offense and seemed utterly unembarrassed as she said, "That is business, *señor*. One must survive."

"Maybe so, but she made me a free offer the other night."

Now it was Saladar who replied: "That is because you are different. She said as much to me. She said, 'This Morgan— he is a *real* man.' "

"Yeah, well, that's swell…but maybe that's what she *wants* you to hear, Luis. And wants *me* to hear through you. The question is, can I trust her?"

Saladar's chin jutted. "As Pedro told you—I would trust her with my life. In fact, I *have*…several times." His eyes narrowed. "Information she had ferreted out for us, it has proved invaluable."

"She made the arrangements at the Hotel Amherst," I reminded him.

"If she had the intentions upon your life, *señor*," Saladar said quietly, "did she not have ample opportunity to act upon them? When you were in her care, and her trust? Would your death have not come sooner, and in less obvious a fashion than by some bomb? No? As you said yourself, your coming here was most accidental. She could not have foreseen your arrival. None of us could."

I leaned back in my chair and took a taste of the coffee. The stuff could make your eyes water. I liked it.

"That," I said, "leaves us with the other hooker—Tami— and that cab driver, whose name I never caught."

Saladar's nostrils twitched and he seemed to grow with

the breath he took. "The driver, *señor*, was my nephew. I will vouch for him gladly."

"Okay. But will you vouch for Tami?"

"Gaita recommended her as a trusted friend."

But a prostitute. A woman who sold herself for money might not hesitate selling somebody else out. On the other hand, I'd met plenty of whores whose morality was superior to a lot of self-proclaimed good people.

"So if we take Gaita's word that Tami's reliable," I said, "we are still left with a great big leaky hole somewhere."

Maria gave me a soft smile. "This house, *Señor* Morgan, it is watertight."

"I'm thinking about *another* house."

"*Señor?*"

"The Mandor Club."

Saladar's eyes were curious now. "This is by the process of elimination, *señor?*"

"In part," I said. "But mostly it's because, as Gaita made clear, the Mandor's a handy little place for picking up tidbits of information you can make pay off. Luis, you said yourself that Gaita has been a top source of information for you... and where did she get that information?"

He shrugged. "The Mandor Club. You are right, *señor.*" Then he shook his head. "But not Gaita, or her friend Tami, either...."

"Still—somebody else could be using it for the same reasons."

"The businesswoman who runs the Club Mandor," Saladar said, "you seem to trust her. She passed your message on to

Pedro, and through him to me. But she would have the perfect opportunity to gather such intelligence."

The military term did not surprise me, coming from this man.

"True," I said. "She may have every room bugged. Hell, they may have film or video cameras going behind one-way glass. But Bunny didn't send the man with the knife."

Saladar's eyes narrowed and his head tilted to one side. "How can you be sure of this?"

"If Maria will pardon a vulgar American expression—you don't shit where you eat. She would hardly sanction a killing in the lobby of her own apartment house."

"Ah," Saladar said, and nodded, accepting that wisdom.

Pedro and Maria had slightly shell-shocked expressions at all this talk of murder and betrayal.

"Anyway," I said, "I like Bunny. I believe her, even if she did try to have me killed a couple times, a long while back."

Once again, they all looked at each other, and tried not to let me know just how crazy they thought their *gringo* guest sounded.

Finally Pedro asked, "This one you killed—"

"I didn't kill him."

"Pardon, *señor*?"

"He fell on his own knife."

"…Yes, I understand. He will not be traced to…to what happened here so recently?" His expression turned woeful, if slightly apologetic. "The militia, they suspect of us of aiding you, *señor*."

"The hitman had no identification on him. It's true I

dumped him in Little Havana, but you're hardly the only Cubans here."

Pedro nodded, sighed, then asked, "What will you do now?"

"Just give it a little time," I said, grinning. "You can't taste the flavor of the stew until it cooks a while."

Maria nodded, agreeing with that advice in general.

Saladar said, "How else may we be of help in your effort?"

"You can start by telling me something."

"Certainly."

"Jaimie Halaquez was a double agent, you said. Who were his contacts in Cuba?"

Saladar shook his head. "That information our *amigo* Jaimie never shared with us. He said that the less we knew, the safer we were—of course, he meant the safer *he* was."

Pedro perked up. "But one time he *did* mention a name. I remember because it was the kind of name you do not forget—Angel Vesta. He seemed unhappy with himself that he had made this...what do you say? This *slip*, and never mentioned it again."

I turned to Saladar. "What does that name mean to you, Luis?"

Saladar gave it a few seconds thought, then said, tentatively, "It might be the one called 'The Angel,' who was at times used to dispatch Castro's enemies. But that is not an uncommon name in Cuba, *Señor* Morgan—Angelo."

"Do you know what this Angel looks like?"

"I do, *señor*. I know also that he is equally adept with the gun and the blade."

I thought about that.

Then I said, "Luis, how would you like to take a walk?"

"Well…uh, certainly, *señor*. You have somewhere in mind?"

"Yeah, I do." I pushed away from the table. "Pedro, Maria, please stay here…and thank you for your hospitality."

Pedro said, "Would you like to stay tonight, *señor*, in the secret place off our bedroom?"

Eyes tight, Saladar said, "It might be wise, *Señor* Morgan. My sources say that this Crowley has distributed your picture to every hotel in Miami."

A little slow off the dime, old Crowley.

"Thank you, Pedro. Thank you, Maria. But I won't place you any further in harm's way tonight than I already have."

Pedro looked slightly forlorn. Or maybe it was just the droopy mustache. He said, "What else may we do to help your cause?"

Funny way to put it, since I was helping their cause.

I took one last sip of coffee, put the cup down on the table and stood up. "You can keep your people alerted for Hala-quez. Somebody should know what charter boats wouldn't mind hiring out for a night trip to Cuba, if the price was right, and the same thing for private aircraft rentals. Make sure anyone you call upon can identify Halaquez by sight, and if he's spotted, they're not to try to take him alone. I'll be in touch."

Saladar and I were on our way out when Pedro stopped us, a hand on my arm.

"*Señor* Morgan," Pedro said hesitantly, "as much as we are honored by your company…and would gladly offer you shelter tonight…it is best you not risk visiting here again. I will give you my phone number and—"

"Don't worry," I said. "I'll call in. No more dropping by. Jaimie Halaquez isn't the only one with a price on his head."

Ten minutes later, Luis Saladar and I were in Domino Park, in the shadows of tall palms that hovered as if eavesdropping.

The park remained deserted, the streets nearby light with traffic, both pedestrian and automotive. I walked the distinguished Cuban freedom fighter to just the right bush, held it back, and gave him a look.

Perhaps out of respect for the dead—*any* dead—he removed his ivory-color plantation owner's hat, then crouched, took a lingering examination, then turned his head and nodded.

Rising, he said, "That is the Angel, *señor*."

"Angel or not, I don't figure he's flying upward tonight."

"No. I would doubt this myself."

We moved away to the sidewalk and strolled slowly.

"Luis, did you have any idea this character was in the States?"

"No. None."

"What does his being here suggest?"

His eyes flared. "Only that what you said before makes sense, *Señor* Morgan—that this must be more important than just the seventy-five thousand dollars that was stolen from my people."

We walked toward where I had parked Bunny's station wagon.

I asked him, "Is there any way you can run a check on who else Halaquez dealt with back home?"

His expression turned grave. "Not without risking getting our own people in difficulty. I can try, *señor*, but I could not press hard for results, this I admit freely."

"Then try your best."

"Very well, *señor*."

He tipped his hat and walked off toward the sounds of Latin music and laughter.

Not that *goddamn good with a gun and blade,* I thought.

Muddy Harris met me in a diner on lower Biscayne Boulevard. He was red-eyed and mussed, his clothes baggier than ever, and when he sat down in the booth opposite me, he made a grimace of disgust and called over for a coffee and pie.

I passed on coffee—I was still buzzed on that Cuban stuff I got at Pedro and Maria's. Sweetened Southern-style iced tea was my excuse for taking up booth space.

"You do know, I haven't hardly slept since you come around, Morgan?"

"Tough."

"Sure, slough it off...*you* don't have anything to lose."

"Just my ass."

He patted his comb-over and his fleshy face made his fold of a smile. "Hell, it's been like that so long with you that you're used to it. Me, I got a business to run. I got mouths to feed."

"And secrets you don't want the cops to know. That's why I got Kirk to alert you in the first place. You live in the same damn limbo world I do."

"No argument there."

"So turn off the self-pity machine. You know I'll take care of you—you'll wind up with a slice of any action."

He let a tobacco-stained grin show through his day-old beard. "Okay, Morgan, okay."

No more posturing. Good.

But Muddy waited until his pie and coffee was in front of him, and the waitress gone, before he said, "For what it's worth, I do have something, but in the interest of fairness, I have to level."

"Interest of fairness? You *are* Muddy Harris?"

"I'm just saying, it wasn't me who ran this down. You know that kid at the Amherst?"

"Sure, the little smart-as-a-whip bellhop."

"That's the one. I mean, I played a role. We kind of angled it out together."

He shoveled some all-American apple à la mode in his pie hole. He talked as he chewed it—not a pretty sight.

"Seems like he thinks you're quite a guy, Morg. Quite… a…guy."

"Some people have taste."

"Seems like he found out *who* you are, too. That you're a living legend and all."

I looked at him and didn't say anything.

"These refugees," he went on, "stick together. They have their own crazy little grapevine." His expression crinkled in thought. "You think I ought to know more about how they work it, Morg? Might come in handy in my trade."

"No. Go on."

Muddy washed some pie and ice cream down with coffee, some of the latter dribbling down his chin like dirty rain. He didn't seem to notice.

"Guess you're right," he said. "That's a whole world of its own."

"Yeah. Wipe your chin."

He did. "Anyway, the kid found two bottles of high-price booze stashed away in that old porter's digs—buried under a pile of junk in the closet of the basement room the geezer used there. Wasn't the grade of stuff he usually swilled down at all—he was more a Muscatel man."

"Less commentary, Mud, more facts."

"Facts? How's this for facts—there were three pawn tickets stuck back there, too, in that closet—one for a cheap portable transistor radio the old fart got a buck for, one for a travel clock he likely swiped out of a room, worth another buck, and another for an old signet ring that had his initials on it, which got him a whole two dollars."

"So he was hard up," I said.

"Just goes to show the old man never had a dime. And what he did have went for cheap wine or booze...that is, until the night that room blew apart. *That* night, from a joint four blocks away? The codger picked up three quarts of the finest hooch...and told the liquor store guy that a hotel guest had just given him a big tip."

"That," I muttered, "is what you get when you pay a drunk in advance."

Muddy blinked at me, freezing between bites of pie. "What, Morgan?"

"If the old porter polished off one of those quarts, *that* explains why he didn't set the timer right."

"Yeah, or maybe you just got lucky, is all."

He finished the pie, swirled the coffee around in the cup, polished it off, and smacked his lips.

"So," Muddy said, "the kid and me start nosing around at what's left of the Amherst Hotel to see who the old man's contact was. We went round and round until finally we get one of those cleaning maids to talk. Seems a few hours before the explosion, she remembers that the old boy asked her to cover for him for a while."

"Did he tell her why?"

"Indeed he did—turns out grandpa had an errand to run. She agreed to help him out, and said he was gone for a couple of hours. When Pops come back, he was acting funny, the maid says, nervous-like, and had something with him that she figured was just another bottle in a brown bag. She nips from her own jug from time to time, so never thought anything much of it."

"Tell me there's more."

"Oh, there's more. After that, it took a whole lot of legwork, but the bellhop and me, we found a place where the old man went for some chili and beer. Seems he was eating when a guy come in, sits next to him and strikes up a confidential sort of conversation. The counterman didn't hear what they were talking about, because the jukebox was blasting away, but when they left, the guy paid for the old boy's eats."

"Get a description?"

"Absolutely," Muddy said, nodding. "The counterman came through. The dining companion was about thirty-five, pretty sharp looking and big for a Cuban type, tall, dark, and nearly handsome. Nearly 'cause of a squashed boxer's nose and a scar kinda like a lightning bolt on his cheek. Not sure which cheek. Anyway, counter guy never saw the big Cuban before, and said he hoped he never did again, 'cause this character looked like the type you didn't mess with…. *Honey!* Honey, do this again, would you?"

Muddy was holding his empty plate out to a passing waitress, and lifting his cup, as well. She stopped, took the plate, and filled the coffee with the pot she was hauling.

When she was gone, Muddy said, "Now here's the kicker. When the big Cuban comes in, he's carrying a package. Only when the two of 'em left? The *old man* had it."

I nodded thoughtfully.

"Got him pegged?" Muddy asked me.

I nodded. *The description fit Jaimie Halaquez, but I didn't tell Muddy that.*

"Ou don't tell me," Muddy said, shrugging. "Send me out for information, but keep the damn contcrt to yourself. That's a good way to get nowhere fast."

I ignored him.

He had a slug of the coffee—it must have been hot because he said, "*Ow*," before asking me, "Maybe you'd like to know something else?"

"Maybe."

"You got that Walter Crowley guy really screwed up. They got a make on the spic who really belonged to those car-wash coveralls. Right now they're figuring you're long gone from the scene."

But it hadn't stopped Crowley from sending my photo around to the hotels.

"Where'd you hear that, Muddy?"

"Big ears, thin walls. It's what makes my world go round."

His new round of pie and ice cream arrived. He dug in.

"Anything on this Consummata dame?" I asked.

"Couple of things." He kept eating.

"Don't let me interrupt," I said.

He swallowed a bite, which meant at least I wouldn't have to watch him masticate while he talked. "Morg, are you aware that this is an older doll?"

"Who?"

"The Consummata!"

"*How* old?"

"Her activities go back to before the war, in Europe. That means, if she started out in her early twenties, you know, real precocious and such like, she's got to be pushing *fifty*, anyway."

"Last time we talked she was a rumor. A legend. Now she's a broad of fifty? What gives, Muddy?"

He shrugged expansively. "Who the hell knows, for sure? But my guess is, she may be a political operative."

"Attached to whom?"

"Who can say? Maybe freelance. Nazis, Allies, Commies, NATO, it's up for grabs. But when you have some special somebody with key information, and that somebody has a kink in their make-up? That's a sweet way to squeeze information out…and ideal blackmail material. Whether it's for money, or military intelligence, it's a great gambit."

Like the Club Mandor, only more so.

I sipped iced tea, kept my tone casual. "You said a couple of things about the Consummata. What else?"

Now he leaned forward, as if suddenly there was something worth being confidential about. "There's a big old house, built in the thirties, one of them stucco mansions, out on Palm Island—near the old Capone estate. Nobody's lived there for years, but it gets rented out, for parties and so on. Word is somebody took it for the next couple months. Paid top dollar to do so."

"Somebody."

"Some woman. Some beautiful woman."

"About fifty?"

"No age. No description. I can dig further and get more, maybe lots more. I can put private eyes on it, if you have the bread. We could stake the place out, see who shows up. Doesn't have to be your Consummata babe. It's a long shot. Longer than any they play at Hialeah. But it's a shot."

Maybe not so long a shot. A mansion on private grounds, out on Palm Island—what better place to install a whips-and-chains playroom or two? Where better to set up an elaborate if temporary dungeon? Elegant enough to suit her clients, secluded enough to let them scream for mercy, or more. What else could the Consummata ask?

"Keep digging," I said.

"And it will be *worth…?*"

Discreetly, I passed him another three hundred bucks off the roll. "Enough?"

He slipped it away. "For now. If you pay for the pie."

"I'll pay for the pie. You just deliver. I'm in no position to go out on the snoop myself."

"I gather that." He glanced at me speculatively. "Anything else you want?"

"Yeah. Get what you can on anybody engaged in traffic with the Cuban mainland. Even suspected activity. Castro shut the casinos down, but I hear he doesn't mind selling the decadent West illegal dope. You know, just to help along the decline of democracy."

Muddy whistled, or anyway tried to. "Brother, you're asking for a lot. That's military ground you're troddin' on. And what isn't military is Mob."

"Information can be bought. That's your business."

He shrugged. "I guess you're right—anything and any-body can be bought, can't it?"

"Not everybody," I said.

CHAPTER EIGHT

I took a circuitous route back through the night to the beginning of the maze Gaita had led me into, reaching into my memory for the right paths and the tunnels that had been part of an abandoned Prohibition brewery.

At intervals I stopped, listened for any feet that might be following my own, wondering whether Walter Crowley would still have kept any of his men posted in the area— Muddy had said the chase had been called off, yet I knew Crowley had only recently sent my photo around to the hotels.

When I was sure I wasn't being followed, I felt my way through the last brick-lined corridor that curved over me like a vault to the nearly invisible door at the end, swung it open on its silent hinges and took a flight of considerably less silent stairs to the top. I laid my ear against the panel, heard nothing, then slipped my fingers in the recessed handle and slid it open.

She was sitting there at the dressing table, her eyes so intent on fixing her makeup, she didn't notice me until I was all the way in. Then she stiffened, snatched a pair of scissors from the tabletop, and spun around in the chair.

"Hello, Gaita," I said.

She took in a soft gasp, laid the scissors slowly down, and allowed a tremor of relief to take her body.

"Morgan," she said, "you bastard. Don't do that again—not *ever*! People, they can get killed that way."

"People can get killed a lot of ways."

That melted her glare, which became a self-conscious smile as she realized the negligee had partially opened, and the suddenly shy little courtesan, with a deft motion of her fingers, folded the lapels one under the other, covering the fullness of her dark-tipped breasts.

"You look like you're dressed for a client," I said.

Her eyebrows rose indignantly and her nostrils flared with pride. "*Señor* Morgan—do not mistake me for the others who work here. Gaita chooses her own company—I am the only one at the Mandor Club with this privilege."

"Any guy you choose would be a lucky devil."

She shook her head and dark curls bounced off her shoulders. "These days I choose to be alone."

"Expensive choice in your trade."

She ignored that, cocked her head and peered at me. "You surprise me, Morgan."

I sat on the edge of a bed. Soft, springy, with a tropical floral spread.

"There aren't many places left for me to go in this town," I said. "The hotels aren't safe. They either have a photo of me, or my room blows up before I get there."

Gaita let seconds drag past before she replied, never taking her eyes from my face. "That's why I have been waiting, Morgan. I knew you would come back."

"I thought you said I surprised you."

"I didn't hear you enter. But I knew you would come. You have questions?"

I glanced at the door, then back to her.

"It is locked," she said. "Even Bunny does not have a key. We have privacy."

That meant a guy could slap her around till she talked, or toss her lovely behind on the lush carpet and ravish her, and with a hand over her mouth, who would know?

Instead I just there sat on the edge of the bed, realizing for the first time how damn tired I was. Somehow a few days had slipped by and there had just been odd fragments of sleep grabbed in even odder places.

With no menace at all, I asked, "Why'd you pick the Amherst, Gaita?"

"Because it was a hotel I could afford. It was not a special place, only out of the way, where I thought you would be safe."

"Nobody suggested it to you?"

"No, *Señor* Morgan. It was my idea only."

"Your friend Tami—you trust her?"

"Completely."

I slipped out of my sport jacket and tossed it on a chair. The .45 in the shoulder sling was showing now. "How'd you make the arrangements?"

"By phone from here."

"I don't see a phone in this room."

"I used Miss Bunny's private line."

And Bunny had assured me her phone wasn't tapped.

"Could anyone have overheard you?"

"I do not think so. The door, it was closed. I spoke softly. With my hand cupped, like this? No, I'm sure there was no one listening."

"Could Tami have passed the information on?"

Gaita gave a slow negative shake of her head, her hair swirling softly about her neck. "Already, I have asked her. *Nada* did she remember mentioning to anyone, not even accidentally. And she knew of the importance of your escape, if not the reasons."

"Uh-huh."

Her chin raised. There was no fear in her voice but I could make out a slight movement in her dark eyes. "Morgan, do you suspect *me*? Do you think that *I*...."

"No," I said.

"You trust me? You believe me?"

"As far as it goes. I just don't think it would've gone down that way."

"What way, *señor*?"

"That simple. If I escaped from the trap at the Amherst—and that's what I'm known for, doll, escaping—they'd know you'd be the first person I asked. They'd probably expect me to torture the truth out of you."

"Then they have not paid attention to the legend."

"What legend?"

"Your legend, Morgan. The legend of the Raider—a man of light who lives in the darkness."

I gave that the snort it deserved. "Maybe Disney will make a TV show out of it."

She smiled then, a lovely, full-lipped smile that was less in response to my little gag than to my belief in her honesty. It was a lovely thank you in an elegant manner, and the tension went out of her like the receding of a wave.

Yet her eyes still held that intense look, probing for

answers. "I did not expect it would be like this, Morgan."

"Like how?"

"Filled with such complication. At first, the mission was only for you to find for us Jaimie Halaquez, and recover our missing funds. Now Bunny has told me of what else has happened—the dead assassin at her apartment building. Even now, she waits for you to call her, sitting there in the office, drinking champagne."

"What's she celebrating?"

"Nothing, *señor*. Quite the reverse. She only does this when she is very much upset."

"Get her up here."

"At once." She stood up, pulled the belt of the negligee tight and went to the door. "Keep it locked behind me, Morgan. I have the key. I'll let myself back in."

"Don't worry about me, kid."

"*Con su permiso*, I will worry about us all."

Then she was gone like a lovely wraith and I lay back on the oversize bed, and folded my hands behind my head, staring at myself in the mirror on the ceiling. If that thing had been a television screen, it would have some wild rerun to play.

Right now I looked like a rerun of myself—on a distant channel that was coming in fuzzy as hell. I looked like ten miles of bad road.

Twenty.

My sport coat and sport shirt and slacks were of high quality, but I'd been in them so long, they were a wrinkled mess and needed a wash. Me, too. Plus a shave.

I closed my eyes for just a moment, and never even heard

them come back. When Bunny shook me, I woke up swearing at myself, because nodding off like that could get me killed.

"Morgan," Bunny said, almost a snarl, "will you please be quiet!"

"Sorry, baby." I didn't realize the .45 was in my hand until I saw them both gaping at it, then I stuck it back in its berth under my left arm.

Bunny shoved me back onto the bed. "Take it easy, cowboy." She gave me an appraising look and let out a disgusted sigh. "You look like hell."

"I feel like hell." I wiped my hand across my face and the bristles damn near hurt my tender little palm. I looked at the hostess of the Mandor Club. "You don't exactly look *your* best either, kiddo."

"Thanks a bunch," she said. "Like they say, with friends like you who needs enemies."

This little adventure was taking its toll on her. Worry lines creased her face, showing through the makeup, and her hair was straggling loose from its formerly artful styling. With those purple streaks, she had a Bride of Frankenstein look as she clutched a handful of note papers, fidgeting with the clips that bound them.

I sat up with a couple of plump pillows propped behind me. "What have you got there, Bunny?"

"First things first." She sat on the edge of the bed. Lithe legs crossed, Gaita was seated at the makeup mirror, but had her back to it, facing us.

"I did what you told me, Morg," Bunny said. "I made inquiries about that murdered client of mine, Dick Best. There was no next of kin and nobody to claim the body. The cops thought it was goddamn big-hearted of me to contribute toward a decent burial, and it didn't seem funny to them at all, when I asked how he was killed."

"How *was* he killed?"

"The usual unidentified blunt instrument that broke his neck. Or it could have a blow from a hand, if the killer was skilled enough."

"A karate chop, you mean?"

She nodded. "They said it was a common mugging technique."

I smirked in disgust. "It really isn't. But that helps the Miami fuzz close the file and not have to look into the matter."

She was nodding again. "Which they didn't, and aren't. They wrote it off as homicide during a burglary gone wrong. They figured Best surprised the robber and got himself killed in the struggle."

"How did the thief get in and out?"

Bunny shrugged. "Either picked the lock or had a skeleton key. There was a fire escape in the hall. Morg, it really is pretty standard stuff."

"Is it? I'd say we're seeing a pattern."

"How so?" Her forehead knitted.

"Somebody likes those single-handed blows. That's how the old porter got it at the Amherst hotel, after he screwed up a certain simple assignment an old *amigo* of yours hired him to do."

Gaita whispered, "Jaimie Halaquez...."

"At least he's consistent," I said. "Give him that much."

Bunny, still on the edge of the bed near me, said, "But the

Cuban boys that were tracking him—in Missouri, Arkansas and Mississippi...*they* didn't die that way."

Gaita said, "Halaquez used a blade. They die slow and painful, those boys, with their insides in their hands."

"Two different kinds of kills," I said, clinically. "Those brave kids were made to suffer—to make them examples, and to send a message back to Little Havana. And they may not have been killed by Halaquez at all."

"What?" Gaita snapped.

It was Gaita's question, but I aimed the answer at Bunny. "They may have been killed *for* him by the Cuban assassin who died in your apartment house lobby. Fitting, he died by the blade."

"You're a cold-blooded bastard," Bunny said with a shiver.

"A breathing one," I said, then went on: "The old man and this Richard Best required efficient kills, not so messy, not so noisy."

The Mandor's madam had a glazed, dazed expression. "So he's still around, our Jaimie...."

"Well," I said, "more like he's back. Bunny, you said first things first. First, was finding out from the cops how Dick Best bought it. What's second?"

Now she smiled; now her eyes took on a twinkle. "Finding out who Dick Best *really* was."

I leaned forward. "*Who*, Bunny?"

"A businessman I was introduced to years ago...but *not* as Richard Best—different last name...Parvain."

Meant nothing to me.

She continued: "Now this goes back a good twenty years,

Morg. I *thought* Dick Best looked familiar, but I couldn't place him—and he looked *more* than twenty years older. Anyway, after seeing the poor S.O.B. stretched out on the morgue tray, well, I came back here and sat down for a good think. Best and I had talked lots of times, in the last year or so—had anything of it meant anything, I wondered?"

"Had it?"

"Maybe. It came back to me that one day, a couple years ago—Best and I were sitting in the bar downstairs, and he gets to telling me about a business of his called Possibilities, Inc. And how it was too bad my husband wasn't around to get in on the ground floor with him again."

"*Again?*"

"Yes, *again*, he said. Morg, at the time, I wondered what he meant by that. But I didn't ask, because you don't pry with clients, or maybe I just got distracted…but at any rate…I never asked him about it."

"Understandable," I granted.

"Then seeing him *dead* like that, suddenly something jarred loose. I remembered something. I remembered that when my husband kicked off, I went through some papers he left, and there was a notation about this Possibilities, Inc."

She gestured with the yellowed packet that she had been holding onto like the railing at a sharp drop-off.

"So I dug them up again," she said, "from my old box of souvenirs from back when we were rich and infamous."

Bunny tossed the moldy sheaf my way, and I picked it up, wondering what answers it might hold.

"They may not make much sense to you," Bunny said.

"That old fox I was married to wasn't much for making notes that the income tax people might follow. But you'll see that he invested ten thousand in a gimmick Parvain invented that was supposed to detect uranium ore from an airplane, instead of working at ground level."

"When was this?"

"Oh, back in those days of all the big strikes in Canada. Up north, everybody and his brother was inventing these gizmos that claimed to sniff out the stuff."

"What are we talking about here," I asked, "glorified Geiger counters?"

She nodded and tendrils blonde and purple bounced. "Exactly right—least as far as I understand it. Nothing ever came of Parvain's deal, or I would have heard about it. My dear departed reprobate husband liked to brag about his scores, but if something didn't pan out, it became a dead issue."

I leafed through the pages, which dated to the mid-1950s, and found the phrase "Possibilities, Inc." twice, among a couple of rows of abstract figuring, and a half-paragraph in an almost illegible scrawl. A heavy check mark went through the whole page, like a memorandum to forget it. "Bunny, you said Best mentioned that it was too bad your husband wasn't in with him *again*. Maybe those Possibilities panned out after all."

She shrugged grandly. "If they did, why didn't Best have a pot to piss in? Unless him living like an old fart on a fixed income was just a front."

"Maybe he was hanging around your club because he

eventually planned to hit you up for a touch—to refinance a business your husband had been part of."

Bunny shook her head thoughtfully. "No, the conversation in question goes back a good couple of years, and Best never mentioned the subject again."

Something wasn't adding up.

I asked, "Where the hell did Best get the kind of money it takes to hang out at the Mandor Club? And how did a nebbish like that even gain entry?"

That stopped her. "Be damned if I know. Somebody on our approved list must have brought him in as an invited guest."

"Is that something you can track?"

"Probably not. Why?"

"Because he was murdered. And anything to do with nuclear physics can be important enough to get somebody killed. It's the only damn lead we have."

Bunny gave me a funny look then, then shook her head.

I said, "What is it?"

"Oh, just something Best said to me, not too long ago. Couldn't be anything important."

"Damn it, who the hell knows *what* might be important, in this damn mess? Spill."

"Well," she said, and paused, thinking back, "I had a birthday party a few weeks ago. Best wasn't here for it, but he called to wish me happy returns. He sounded half in the bag, and I was a little potted myself, so…"

"So?"

"So he said he was sorry he didn't have a present for me,

but he'd stop by with something when he got a chance. And then what he said after that was weird...."

"Weird how?"

"Weird and then some—Morg, he said that if anything happened to keep him from visiting the Mandor Club again, I should expect to receive a late birthday present."

I frowned. "Has anything shown up? In the mail, or from a shipping firm?"

She shook her head. "Nothing."

"Well, keep a goddamn sharp eye out. Do you think Best thought his life was in danger?"

Her shrug was almost comically exaggerated. "I don't know. Like I said, he sounded drunk. And I *was* drunk. I'm really not sure I should be trusting my memory on this subject...."

"Perhaps," Gaita said from her seat on the sidelines, where she'd been quietly taking it all in, "Tango might know something of this."

"Tango, kitten? Who's that?"

But it was Bunny who answered. "Just one of the girls, Morg. Real name's Theresa Prosser. Gaita's right—this Best character, or Parvain or whoever he was, was pretty smitten with Tango. Even took her out to supper a few times."

"Is she here now?"

"No! Look, Morgan, the last thing we need to do is get anybody *else* involved in this mess..."

"Let me worry about that. Tell me about Tango. How special was she to Best?"

Bunny was rolling her eyes. "Christ, Morg, don't make more out of it than what I've already told you! Best just seemed to prefer Tango's company, if she was available."

"Meaning, Best might have told her something that he didn't tell you or any of the other girls."

Bunny seemed openly annoyed now. "This is a business like any other—employees get days off, and this is hers. She's probably at the Vincalla Motel. Goes there and sits around the pool all day, when she's not working. At night she reads or watches TV. Quiet girl."

"Is there a boyfriend in the picture?"

Now Bunny seemed strangely amused. "Gaita, why don't *you* break it to him?"

Gaita made a resigned gesture with her shoulders. "Tango, she is a lovely woman. One of the loveliest and most in demand here at the Mandor. But she does not like the men."

"Funny game to go into, then. So, she's a lesbian?"

"No. She is…how you say…frigid."

Bunny said, "Tango says the act of sex is no more exciting, or meaningful, to her than brushing her teeth or using the john."

I frowned. "What, so she puts on an act for her clients?"

"No. She takes great pleasure in having them work hard to please her while she remains bored. It's her way of feeding her hatred for men."

"Why is she popular, then?"

Gaita took that one: "Because she is very beautiful, *señor*."

Yeah, and what man doesn't think he's just the right guy to melt an ice queen?

I asked, "Yet she went out on…what, *dates* with this Best character?"

"Him she did not mind," Gaita said. "He was more the father to her. My guess is, they never did the act of sex together."

Bunny cut in: "To what degree she can put up with men, Tango prefers older ones, like Best. Younger men, closer to her own age, she has a supreme contempt, even hatred, for."

"Why in hell?"

Again, it was Gaita who responded: "It is because of her older brother, *Señor* Morgan. He is dead now. Because he raped her. And she killed him."

"Okay, I'm starting to get the picture."

"This is why she left Cuba, *señor*. To flee the police for this crime, but it was really self-defense."

I nodded. "How old is she now?"

"She is twenty."

"Brother," I whispered under my breath. "How long has she been at the Mandor?"

Bunny took that one: "Four years," she said, too casually.

"That's rape, too, you know," I told the madam pointedly. "Statutory rape."

"She had papers saying she was twenty-one when she came here," Bunny said. "I take my girls at their word."

"Even when you know they're lying."

"Excuse me if I don't take morality lessons from Morgan the Raider."

I raised a hand to quell any argument.

Then I crawled off the other side of the bed, got to my feet and tried to shake the tiredness out of my body.

"Okay," I told them, "I'm going to speak to Tango, then I'm coming back here. In the meantime, Bunny, you rack that memory of yours for anybody else who might have been involved with Parvain and your hubby in that Possibilities company. Come up with *somebody* we can track down."

Her eyes flared. "Morgan, damn it, that was *years* ago."

"Phone operators are the best tracers of missing persons in the world. Let your fingers do the walking—just don't bust a nail."

Bunny came over and touched my arm. Suddenly the good-looking old broad had what seemed to be a genuine look of concern. "Going to that motel—aren't you taking a big chance?"

"Who isn't?"

"Morgan…"

The tone of Bunny's voice made me meet her eyes. "What, kiddo?"

She whispered, though surely Gaita could hear. "Tell me …please…what did you do with that…that *person* who was killed at my building?"

"I left him in Domino Park behind some bushes."

She had the expression of a startled deer. "There was nothing about it in the papers."

"Yeah, I know. Kind of curious, isn't it?"

Her mouth was a tight line now. "Morgan…sometimes you frighten me."

"Just sometimes?"

Then I got a closer glimpse of myself in the dressing table mirror.

"No wonder," I said. "You think maybe I could scare up a shower and a shave around here someplace?"

Bunny didn't answer me—maybe this simple indignity was the last straw.

But Gaita came over, took my arm and gave me one of her funny, sexy grins. "Why, of course, *señor*—we attend to all of a man's needs here at the Mandor Club."

She was good as her word.

I was halfway through the shower, the spray like hot little friendly needles that were bringing me to life even as the steam soothed me and uncoiled muscles that were tight with stress and too little sleep. I was washing my hair with a bath bar, eyes tight shut as soapy water trailed down my face, when I heard the shower stall open.

Gaita slipped inside and she was naked, with her hair pony-tailed back, and her makeup already washed off, a fresh, youthful girl but no kid, not with breasts so full and high, their dark nipples taut, not with that supple belly where a little whisper of dark hair worked its way from her navel down to gradually expand into the lush dark tangle of the delta between her legs, the rest of her a coppery smoothness that the water seemed to love, to caress, to turn her into a gleaming goddess, pearled with moisture, her parted lips dripping water down like nectar flowing from a goblet.

She began to soap my front, lathering up my chest hair, then lathered lower and had she spent any more time down there, we'd have been finished before we started; but then her arms slipped behind me as she soaped my back while the front of her was pressed to me, the breasts splayed against me.

"Gaita…no…I'm…."

She covered my mouth with hers, lips with a full plumpness that seemed to consume mine, and over the hammering of the shower and the splash at our feet and the gurgle of the drain, she drew away from me and said, "You are *not* married. Did you not tell me so yourself? You have not consummated the act. You do *not* betray her. You do not."

This time *I* kissed *her*.

We moved away from the spray of the showerhead, to the rear of the stall where she pushed me against the wall like a suspect, but she did not interrogate me, she went down on her knees, she went down on me, and for a moment I thought of Kim, but just a moment, because then the Cuban kitten was rising and turning and leaning against the wall with her hands flat against the tile, glancing back at me with sultry insistent invitation, offering the rounded cheeks of the most perfect posterior that fool Castro ever banished from his country.

And not doing something about it would have been goddamn insulting, so I entered her and she said, "*Si!*" with every stroke, grinding back at me in a rhythmic sexual samba that required no music but our heavy breathing and the percussive insistence of the shower.

We wound up on the floor of the bathroom on a fluffy little rug, first with her riding me, her eyes shut dreamily, her mouth beaming with bliss, rocking, grinding, rocking, then with me on top, stabbing her sweetly, and when she came, she cried out in a language neither Spanish nor American, but I understood it perfectly.

Finally I was sitting, out of breath, on the lid of the can, feeling like I was the one who'd been ravished. She had already disposed of the rubber she'd so stealthily slipped onto me, practiced doxy that she was.

Now she stood and toweled herself off, shamelessly at ease with her body, and then in the mirror carefully applied her lipstick, put on a touch of eye makeup, and undid the ponytail and shook all that hair like the lioness mane it was, looking at herself, pleased with what she saw.

"I told you," she said into the mirror but speaking to me, "that *I* do the choosing."

She turned to her exhausted conspirator and said, "You are not married. You will not be married until the marriage it is consummated. This is no sin, *señor*. You remain pure."

That was a hell of a way to look at it.

On the other hand, she was the first woman I'd been with since I married Kim.

And maybe it didn't hurt to stay in practice.

CHAPTER NINE

The taxi let me out on the corner and I walked the rest of the way to the Vincalla Motel. Traffic had dwindled and—while the lights of Miami Beach still lit the sky across the bay—this side was quiet and sleepy, the only activity around being restaurants and nightclubs catering to the singles scene.

I looked like just another Miami swinger, Bunny having come up with a black sport jacket, charcoal sport shirt and black slacks for me. I had requested black sneakers, wanting to keep the sound of my footsteps minimal, and the madam of the house had come through for me on that score as well.

Between Bunny and Gaita, I could hardly have any complaints about the service at the Mandor Club.

I skirted the motel office out front, crossed the lawn that circled the pool, and headed toward the room I'd been told was Tango's, down on the right.

At the opposite end, a party was going on, split between two rooms, the blare of a hi-fi playing rock 'n' roll and raucous drunken laughter covering the sound of my feet on the concrete walk. The motel's parking spaces, outside the bottom tier of rooms, were filled, license plates about evenly divided between local and out-of-state. With the exception of three rooms up top and four below, all windows were darkened, Tango's among them.

For a second I stopped, checked behind me, and slow-scanned the area toward the street to see if anyone was silhouetted against the street-lamp and traffic glow. Five feet away was Tango's room, and I could see the windows curtained with no light bleeding through at all.

If Bunny was right, the man-hating hooker was probably just asleep—the motel was where she went to relax and cool it. But I still couldn't shake the feeling that there was something wrong with the play.

You can't call it instinct, because it's learned; but it's nothing mental, strictly physical, as the back of your neck prickles and your belly tightens and your eyes narrow and your mind becomes a resonating space where caution calls to you in vague yet not uncertain terms.

So I just stood there, looking around again and sorting out the details until my inner warning system found the flaw for me.

Tango didn't have a car. She always traveled by cab, Bunny had said.

Yet all the car slots were filled.

Maybe some of the partygoers down at the other end weren't guests at the Vincalla, and the overflow had filled up some extra slots.

But down here on this very quiet end of things, a blue Mustang convertible was parked in the stall right outside Tango's room, and its hood was still very warm. Hot.

I snaked the .45 out, cocked the hammer back and took a run at the door, smashing it open with a kick, then rolling inside just as the *phut* of a silenced gun poked two fingers of light directly over my head. I scrambled to my knees, brought the .45 up, and a foot kicked the gun out of my hand.

But I got that hand on my would-be assailant's other leg, yanked hard, and a cursing, flailing heavyweight came down on top of me, the rod in his fist smashing against my back and shoulders trying to find my skull.

I gave him just enough leeway to think he had me nailed, then drove my head up against the point of his chin and, when he reeled back, grabbed him between the legs and squeezed so hard the scream that started in his throat never got anywhere, choking off into an anguished sob as he jack-knifed forward with incredible pain.

That put me over onto my back, and I was under him, with no idea where my .45 had got to, and for all the pain he was in, he did still have that silenced rod in his mitt, he'd managed to hold onto it, so I glommed onto his gun hand before he could get his pain in check, and twisted my grip on his wrist, thumb slipping under the butt of the gun into the fleshy palm, digging my thumbnail in, hoping to make his grasp go away, but instead in the struggle I again heard that little *phut* and a bullet angled up and into him, his sob whistling off into a throaty rattle that had bubbles in it.

I pushed him off me, still wondering where the .45 had got to, and moved to where the door stood open, and peeked out to see if anybody had heard the noise of the struggle. But there was nothing out there, just the laughter and rock music of that party down the way.

Luck was still with me, it seemed.

Only it wasn't—I never figured on a second man. Never figured the guy I'd tangled with, who was still giving off his death rattle on the floor, had a friend with him, a friend who would quietly wait in the darkness of the bathroom to see how the fight between his partner and the intruder turned out.

Those well-honed instincts had let down, and the only sign luck was still with me was when the karate chop missed the back of my neck, because I was just starting to turn, the blow hitting between my shoulder blade and spine, sending pain through me like a hot spear and maybe cracking or even breaking a rib, but not killing me, not hardly.

And when he shoved me into that open door, rattling my teeth and banging my head, damn near putting my lights out, he didn't take time to try another karate chop—maybe he knew enough about me to want to avoid any direct confrontation—and just rushed past me.

In the second I needed to recover, I saw that almost handsome face fly by me, with its squashed nose and lightning bolt scar.

Jaimie Halaquez.

My .45 was M.I.A., but Halaquez had a gun in his hand, another silenced automatic that went *phut phut*, sending two chunks of doorframe exploding into splinters and flying into my face.

Then he was in the Mustang, squealing out, and flashing a white grin of *adios* at me—I wasn't dead, but he'd beaten me. He had beaten me.

Me, with no gun. I didn't even have a goddamn *car*, having returned Bunny's station wagon.

Shit!

The only saving grace was nobody seemed to have heard or seen a thing. Only silenced shots had been fired, and the hand-to-hand had been brief if brutal.

But why hadn't Halaquez waded in to help his partner?

Hadn't wanted to risk exposing himself, I guessed. He'd figured his crony would take me out, no trouble, and if not, Jaimie boy would deal with me.

Heaving a disgusted sigh evenly divided between the unkindness of fate and my own stupidity, I went back into the still dark room, shoved the door shut, propped a chair against it, and flipped on the light.

Tango was sprawled on the bed.

What had originally been a pretty face was now a battered mass of welts and bruises; a strip of two-inch wide adhesive covered her mouth, another strip binding her hands behind her. The remnants of her pajama tops were tossed on the floor, and she was naked to her waist, pert perfectly-formed breasts exposed, but there was nothing remotely sexy or erotic about it.

Not unless you were a sick son of a bitch.

I felt my face tighten as I took in the ugly red pits that had been burned into the smooth tanned flesh of her stomach and breasts, the mark of lit cigarettes in the hands of her interrogators. I wished I could have taken longer with the bastard on the floor, given him a slower, more painful send-off to hell.

And when I finally nailed Halaquez, I would remember this beautiful body made hideous.

But at least she wasn't dead—not yet, anyway.

She *was* unconscious, probably a blessing at the moment, her pulse light and unsteady. When I yanked the tape from her mouth, she never even stirred. I cut her wrists free and released her arms, retrieved my .45 from under a chair, then went over for a better look at the dead man.

He wasn't as big as Halaquez, but larger than the average Latin—Jaimie did not seem lacking in brutal henchmen from his native land. As the gurgling I'd heard had indicated, the bullet had caught the prick in the throat and exited at the back of his neck. The gun was still in his hand.

I went through his pockets, found nothing except his car keys, some loose cash, and a half-empty pack of cigarettes. His clothes were all well worn with labels common to stores in every big city, and the touch of the professional was there in every detail. Nothing but his basic appearance identified him as a Cuban, with or without a green card.

The drawers of the motel-room dresser were open, and had been tossed, but not much was there—no sexy working clothes, just casual stuff and underthings. She'd arrived, apparently, with a single suitcase, and what was left of it was shredded over by the wall, a blade having gutted its lining. Next to the dead suitcase was the woman's emptied handbag, by a scattering of the usual female junk, the bag apparently tossed there in disgust.

Whatever Halaquez had been looking for, he hadn't found it in this room. His next step had been to try to squeeze it out of the girl the hard way.

But now a peculiar little factor had popped up.

Tango wouldn't have been the type to keep quiet under

that kind of treatment. If she had anything to say, she would likely have talked, not been subjected to beating and burning.

That left just one answer. Whatever Halaquez wanted from her, she either didn't have…

…or didn't *know* she had.

Yet somebody thought *she had it, or that she maybe* knew *something*.

I picked up the bedside phone with my handkerchief, dialed the police, told them where to find the trouble, and to send an ambulance.

"I'm a guest here at the Vincalla Motel," I told the dispatcher.

"Sir, what is your name?"

"John Smith. I'm sure you'll find it on the register."

I hung up.

There was nothing more that John Smith, Good Samaritan, could do for Tango now. I rubbed my handkerchief on anything else I might have touched, gave the corpse one last dirty look, then shut the light off, eased out of the room and got back out to the street.

From the south I could hear the wail of sirens over the rock 'n' rolling partyers.

We were in Bunny's office now. She looked damn fetching for an older broad in a gold lamé halter top and matching loose pants. She was behind her desk where a .38 was serving as a paperweight on those ancient papers of her husband's that she'd shared with me earlier.

But her face was again showing her years, as the dismay

over what had happened to Tango mingled with fear generated by the events of recent days.

She said, "But why *torture* her, Morgan? What did they want? What did she know?"

I was seated across from her. "No idea. She was out when I got there, and still out when I split. What did the hospital say?"

Bunny sighed. "Severe concussion and suspected skull fracture. She hasn't regained consciousness." The madam covered her face with her hands, her shoulders limp. When she looked up her eyes were misty and tired. "She's on the critical list."

"Think the cops can connect her to you?"

"Maybe not right away, but they will. She's always used the address of her family, on the north end, and all that's left there is her father, and they won't get anything from that drunken bum. She paid his bills and went up there a couple times a month, but all he knows is that she worked someplace in Miami. She told him she was a waitress."

"A waitress who could pay all his bills?"

"Reprobate parents getting their bills paid by their kids, Morg, don't ask a lot of questions."

"Good point. Otherwise she stayed here at the Mandor?"

Her shrug was grandiose. "Where else? She has her own room, like the others. My girls are welcome to live here full-time, if they like. Most, like Tango, have an apartment or motel room somewhere, to get away on their days off, at least."

"Let's see her room."

Bunny sat and watched me, her mouth tight. "Morgan…I think it's time to let this thing end."

"Look…"

Her expression beseeched me. "Look at all you've brought on, since you got here! Two men dead. And we have a girl who may die because of it."

"Not my doing, Bunny. And I didn't bring *anything* on. It was already here."

"You can't deny you've stirred things up."

So I dropped the bomb on her.

"Bunny—one of the two men I tangled with in her motel room? Not the one who bought the farm, but…the *other* one?"

"Yes?"

"He was Jaimie Halaquez."

Her expression fell and all the blood drained from her face.

Silently, I rose, slipped off the sport jacket, draped it over the back of my chair, then I slipped off the sport shirt and turned my back to her.

Showed her the nasty welt there, a welt about the size and shape of the side of a human hand, swung as a weapon

With my back still to her, I said, "If I hadn't moved a fraction of a second before he struck the blow, that would have hit my neck. And I'd be on a slab next to your old pal Dickie Best."

She said nothing. She sat staring at the sheaf of papers and the revolver playing paperweight on top of them.

In the meantime, I got back into my shirt and jacket. "I figure you have a doc on call, right?"

She frowned in confusion, then nodded.

"Well, could you call him, and get him over here to check me out, in between passing out penicillin tablets? I think maybe Halaquez busted a rib for me. I could use taping up, and some decent damn drugs."

She swallowed, nodded, and reached for her phone.

When she hung up, she said, "Half an hour."

"Cool. While we're waiting, let's go see Tango's room."

Tango lived in relative simplicity. Her clothes were few, if expensive, the opposite of the casual things in the dresser at the motel—these were working clothes, or in some cases, evening wear. After all, she'd been known to date Richard Best.

"She didn't meet johns in this room," I said.

Bunny said, "No. Each of the girls has her own living quarters, modest but her own. You've been in Gaita's. There are suites designed for entertaining guests—the girls share those. Those spaces are assigned when the client and a hostess are matched up."

That explained the simplicity of a room bare of decorations except for two bowls of artificial flowers and a few abstract paintings of the starving artist variety. The only expensive item was a 21-inch color television set nestled in one corner with a battered comfy armchair before it. Tango's small desk held a few cancelled bills, a dictionary, and a dozen historical romances with bodice-bursting damsels and swashbuckling bare-chested heroes on the front—everybody had their fantasies, even a woman who represented other people's fantasies.

Her irritation with me ever more obvious, Bunny said, "Well? Does it send you any messages?"

I ignored her and went to the closet again. Tango's shoes were neatly aligned in a rack with a matching handbag above each. Out of curiosity, I took the handbags down one by one and looked in them. Each one had some odd toiletry items along with a few coins. One had a letter from an old friend sent to her home address, four months ago, full of chatter about the other girl's marriage and children in a more normal life than Tango had managed so far. I noted the street number of Tango's house, and put the letter back.

But the blue bag held the kicker.

In the side pocket was a worn-edged picture that I held out for Bunny to see.

Softly, she said, "My God…it's Jaimie Halaquez."

"I thought Tango didn't take to men. Especially younger men."

Bunny frowned and handed the picture back. "That photo doesn't mean she flipped over him or anything."

"Hell, Bunny, it's the only photo she has."

"So?"

"You ever notice them together? Was Halaquez a client of hers?"

"Morgan, in this business, it's a business to be together. You know already that he was a client here. Sure, he knew her, but he liked variety too much to single any girl out. Understand, this Halaquez was a real self-styled stud."

"And an S & M freak. Don't leave that out."

"Yes, and not all of the girls were willing to go down that

road. So that does narrow it for you. Within reason, if the money was right? Tango was willing."

"In other words, two to tango."

"Very funny."

"Maybe," I said, thinking out loud, "she had the same kind of yen and you didn't know about it. Some women who were abused as young girls develop their own weird kinks."

The madam didn't argue that point—she knew all too well how many weird sexual byways there were for human beings to go down.

"Maybe," Bunny said, "Tango had a thing for Halaquez, at least enough to hang onto his picture."

"Do you know if she ever saw Halaquez outside of the club?"

"I don't," she admitted.

"But we *do* know she sometimes dated her clients outside the Mandor's doors. Dick Best a case in point."

Bunny nodded, but then contradicted it with a head shake. "If Tango *did* date Halaquez, she never mentioned it. Nobody asks too many questions around here. And Dick Best is the only one I know of that she dated away from the club."

I stuck the photo in my pocket and put the handbag back on the shelf. "Think I can beat Gaita out of her room tonight? She can stay here in Tango's room instead."

"I'm not crazy about you staying around, Morgan. You're trouble."

"You're telling me? That's why I want that handy back exit out of her room. Look, I can't risk a hotel and the cops might spot me on a park bench."

She sighed, a world-weary one, but then she gave me a little smile that said all was forgiven. Or most, anyway. "All right, Morg, I'll arrange it."

"Thanks."

"Although Gaita may prefer sharing her room with you, to giving it up."

"She and I can negotiate that. Just make sure she knows I'm coming."

"Somehow," Bunny said archly, "I think she'll *know* when you're coming. Morgan...what about Tango? How much heat is this liable to raise here at the Mandor?"

"And here I thought you were concerned about Tango as a friend."

She *whapped* me on the arm—sort of a friendly *whap*, but a *whap*. "Bastard," she said.

I grinned at her, shrugged. "My bet is that the cops will call it an attack by a sadist that was interrupted by someone who heard her yell. What happened is obvious enough—somebody tortured her. Whether to get information out of her, or just for the jollies, that's in the eye of the beholder. It'll be easy enough to understand why her rescuer would call the cops but get the hell out."

But I was wrong. The cops didn't call it anything at all. The next morning there would be no mention of it in the papers, nor any of the guy who had fallen on his knife in the lobby of Bunny's apartment house.

Right now, of course, I didn't know that. We went to Bunny's office to wait for the doctor. We sat on her handsome leather couch, plumped up with big plush pillows, over which loomed that paisley wall hanging.

Her half-lidded eyes regarded me. "You think I'm a cold-hearted bitch, don't you?"

"Not really," I said. "I think you're a decent enough dame. I understand why you don't want to risk what you've got going here. I know you care about your girls."

Her expression softened. There was real warmth in those dark blue eyes.

When she kissed me, it came as a surprise. Not a bad one, either, but a surprise.

"You know," she said, "I don't mind that you're married. Not at all. A lot of married men do business here."

"Yeah, you *do* know I make a policy of not paying?"

"I didn't say anything about charging you, Morg. Anyway, I kind of owe you one…I did try to have you killed, once or twice."

I kissed her and it was starting to get somewhere when a knock came at her door, and a muffled voice said, "It's Doc Wilson, Bunny! You in there?"

I took my tongue out of her mouth and my hand off her right breast and said, "Maybe I should get my busted rib taped up before we take this any farther…."

A thundering rain had driven everybody indoors and was beginning to turn the streets into sluiceways. The cabbie who had picked me up reluctantly let me out a block from where I asked to be dropped, clearly wondering what kind of nut would want to wade through a night like this one in a ramshackle neighborhood slated for rebuilding when the city got tired of looking at it.

Tango may have possessed an exotic queenly beauty, perfect for her to play Cleopatra in the movies, but she sure hadn't been raised in pretentious surroundings. The house she grew up in was a relic of those days when the boom hit Miami, then collapsed to leave the memory of inflated money behind by way of unpainted siding and sagging verandas. The wind had blown two aged wicker rockers onto their backs on the porch, and kept the torn screen door slamming on its hinges, like the face of the house kept getting slapped. The noise didn't seem bother anybody, though.

I stepped across the litter of soggy newspaper and leaves plastered to the porch floor, rapped on the door, and waited. I did it again without getting an answer, said the hell with it, and tried the knob. The door swung in limply, half-loose from the frame, and—when I closed it again—sighed with creaking release.

The smell was like a foul fog in the air. Rotted garbage was the base, somewhere a dirty toilet added its bouquet while whiskey and beer fumes gave it that certain tang. The only occupant downstairs was an unshaven, dead-to-the-world guy in his middle fifties who was sprawled out on the couch, like Lizzie Borden's papa waiting to get the axe.

The sleeper reeked of booze, two empty bottles on the floor beside him, his half-naked belly poking through a split shirt and his pants held together by an old army belt with the zipper wide open. A half-dozen pension check stubs were on the table at one end of the couch—the name typed on them: George L. Prosser.

Tango's old man.

No great surprise there. Scratch a whore, find a no-good father.

I tried shaking him awake, but it was no good. He didn't even make sounds of protest or even of reflexive awareness. The bum would be out a pretty long time yet.

I went through the downstairs rooms, kicking my way through the mess, then upstairs to what used to be the bedroom level.

Two rooms were totally empty.

One was as much of a mess as those downstairs. The fourth had been locked, but somebody had broken it open. This one had been neat and clean until somebody had ripped it into little pieces.

So this was Tango's room—the one she returned home to, once or twice a month.

There hadn't been much to strip out of the single dresser or the closet. Her clothes were out-of-style teenage things from school days long ago, along with some paint-spattered (though otherwise clean) dungarees and a few sweaters. The stuffing had been pulled out of the antique mohair chair, the mattress torn to shreds, and the flimsy little desk knocked to splinters with the old letters and notepaper it held scattered all over the floor.

Two pictures had been yanked from the wall and their backs removed, one ornamental top knocked off a bedpost to make sure they were solid, and the linoleum rug ripped into hunks to see if anything had been hidden under it.

But at least it gave me an idea of what somebody was looking for. It had to be small and it had to be flat. And it had to be important enough to kill for.

They had looked for it here, whatever it was.

Then they had gone after Tango herself.

So far they hadn't found it, and she hadn't given it to them, probably because she had no idea what the hell her torturers were after.

I left everything as it was and went back downstairs. George Prosser was still motionless on the couch, his breath burbling between his lips. He had pissed his pants without knowing since I last saw him, a few minutes ago. Well, it was cold in the house, on this rainy night, so maybe it would keep him warm a while.

Not that hard to figure, why Tango left home.

When I reached the section where the Club Mandor operated, I found the opening to the maze that led to Gaita's room. I had the route so well sketched out in my mind, I didn't need a light anymore.

I carefully went up the stairs, slid the door open, stepped inside, and closed it with a flick of my hand.

The only illumination came from the partially opened bathroom door, a pale yellow glow that was enough to barely outline the shapely female figure on the bed.

I felt a twinge of annoyance because as pleasant a bedroom companion as she would make, I really didn't want Gaita to be here tonight. I was tired, I had thinking to do, and being with me right now was inherently dangerous for her.

But what the hell, it *was* her room, and there was no trace of anything but affection in my voice, as I said, "You asleep, Gaita?"

"No, Morgan, I'm not asleep...."

But it wasn't Gaita at all.

It was another lovely dark-haired woman, with a revolver leveled at my gut.

Kim Stacy.

My wife.

CHAPTER TEN

The gun in Kim's hand lowered—maybe the little automatic was meant for *anyone* who came in Gaita's secret door, and not me specifically.

Then a lush smile blossomed on that lovely oval with the violet almond-shaped eyes.

"Hello, husband."

She'd been resting on top of that bed, waiting—*for me?*—and curled up with a panther-like poise, a luscious doll who made a simple short-sleeve pink blouse and short black shift skirt with no nylons into something wildly sensual. Yet the only real effort to look fetching at all came from the scarlet-red painted toenails showing in the open-toed sandals that matched the red of her full, moist lips.

"Hello, wife," I said.

The gun tumbled from her hands onto the bed and she came off it and into my arms and our kiss was a devouring thing, the greeting of two starving creatures too long away from the table.

I held her to me with one arm around her waist and my other hand touching the dark tresses, cut shorter now, just to her chin, not her shoulders, and the sun streaks were gone. Her features were the same, perhaps some lines of worry around her eyes, for her husband, I hoped, and she was searching my face, studying it as one of her hands was splayed against my back and the other dug into my hair gripping, stroking, gripping, stroking.

I glanced meaningfully at the bed, and she drew away, still in my arms but shaking her head. "Not now, my love. Not here. Not in this place."

I didn't let go of her, said, "Who cares where?" and I kissed her again, and my tongue got insistent about it, and hers held its own, until the moment came when she pulled away, out of my arms now, and found her way to Gaita's dressing table stool and sat here. Her eyes directed me to the bed, but only to sit there. Only to sit.

And perhaps that reminder of Gaita played a part in why I didn't just throw her down on that bed—that this room and the nearby bathroom with shower stall marked the site of my sole failing in staying true to her, over these long months....

That, and the grave expression that had erased her look of love and pleasure at seeing me again.

So I sat on the edge of the bed across from where she perched at the dressing table, her back to its mirror.

"We may not have a lot of time," she said. "I'm breaking every rule in the B-4 book just being here."

She was with the CIA's B-4 Intelligence, Section A.

"We have to talk, Morg. There's so much you need to know. And you have things to tell *me*, too."

I gave her half a smile. "Doll, you want to go the foreplay route, that's fine with me."

"Not foreplay, darling. Fore*warning*—you are in dangerous waters, even for you. This Halaquez inquiry...I'm breaking deep cover to warn you off of it. Let the pros handle it."

I grinned at her. "Back together only a few minutes, and you're already insulting me? Reminds me of when we first met. How'd you know to find me here?"

But she didn't grin back or smile—her expression remained somber, and her forehead was creased with concern. "Never mind any of that now. Will you just listen? For these many months…almost a year, Morgan…I've been doing my own investigating within the agency. It's risky and I've tossed protocol out the window. If what I've done is ever found out, I won't just lose my pension, I may face treason charges."

I stood, and I made a crooking finger at her. "Come over here. I won't rape you—I promise. But I need to be close to you."

She didn't have to think about it. Just did trust me, however much a horny son of a bitch she knew me to be—she knew that more than anything, I loved her, and wouldn't dishonor her.

We arranged ourselves on the bed, with pillows propped up on the headboard behind us, and with my arm around her, so that when she spoke to me, I could feel the warmth of her breath. Curled up against me like a kid. Now and then I would interrupt her to crush those cushiony lips in the gentlest, friendliest way, never pressing to where things might get away from us. She clearly didn't want that.

"Let's start," she said, "with what you've been up to. I've tracked you, your every move. I could have been in touch with you any number of times—we were in the same city three times, once San Francisco, again in Boston, and then in New York."

"Why didn't you…?"

"I'm being watched. You must know I went to bat for you. I told my superiors I'd witnessed that old pal of yours confess to complicity in the robbery, heard with my own ears his claim to have taken possession of the entire forty-mil boodle." Her mouth tightened bitterly. "But it was just like you warned me, in the plane, before you jumped."

They figured that the in-name-only marriage vows Kim and I took had turned into the real thing, working undercover together. Under covers *was their assumption, and though we never consummated our marriage, we* had *fallen in love, hadn't we?*

I said, "Your bosses figured that a wife would say or do anything for her husband. As simple as that."

She sighed and nodded, nestled against me, one full breast mashed against my chest. She smelled great—no perfume, just a freshly scrubbed scent.

"It was all I could do," she said, "all I could *risk*, to conduct an after-hours, off-the-books investigation. There are two things that I think will shock you. First, on the money-truck heist—"

"There was an inside man. A government traitor."

The natural long lashes were tiny whips as she blinked at me. "*What?* How did you—"

"The route the armored car took from the Washington mint to New York was top secret. Standard operating procedure would be to have at least three such routes, and alternate in a shifting, unknowable pattern. Same goes for when the truck would leave and be scheduled for arrival. Also, the knowledge that this particular shipment would be forty million in common bills, nothing over a fifty. You don't pull down a score like that without inside information."

She was smiling, more admiration than love in it, and her head was shaking. "You are one smart bastard, Morgan. You've known this all along?"

"Oh, only since the day I heard they were after me. But for me, it's a theory. You sound like you're passing along a fact."

The almond eyes narrowed. "I can't say that it's a fact of the kind that might hold up in court—not yet. And the people I talked to are unlikely to go on the record. But let me just say that you're in the right city for us to be having this conversation."

I frowned. "Sounds more likely to be a Washington D.C. conversation than a Miami one."

"No, Miami all the way....Morg, I believe that forty mil was a very inside job. That it was a CIA black op."

"*What?*"

Now she *had* surprised me.

"That money," she said, "was earmarked for the Cuban freedom fighters' cause. Just a few years ago, remember, the Company was funding and shaping the efforts to take Castro down, but it was strictly *sub rosa*—the White House starting with Vice President Nixon and on to both JFK and his attorney general brother knew all about it, from exploding cigars designed to kill Castro to the secret commando training camps in the Florida Everglades...all of it top secret."

I was ahead of her now. "But then the Bay of Pigs came along, and the Cuban Missile Crisis, and—"

"And the president shot down in a Dallas street, and all of the plans to assassinate Castro and invade Cuba became a political embarrassment, a Cold War liability. If Castro had JFK killed, nobody wanted to say so—at best, it meant that embarrassing proof we'd been plotting to kill a foreign leader would come out, and at worst that a hailstorm of nukes would fall all over the world."

"Wait," I said, and I touched her hand, squeezed it. "The money-truck heist—that was well *after* the Kennedy hit. All of these Cuba plans would have been shut down by then."

She nodded. "Yes, but there were rogue elements within the Company that still wanted those efforts to move forward. That forty-million-dollar heist was a last ditch effort by those forces to fund an invasion of Cuba by Cuban exiles."

"Actually a noble cause," I said, then rolled my eyes. "All except for the part where Morgan the Raider gets framed for the heist."

"That was a genius stroke," Kim said, with a wry half-smile. "Somebody must have enlisted your crew and either painted it as a money-making effort, or possibly brought them in as patriots. You were all highly decorated heroes of the European theater."

"They would have come aboard as patriots," I said, "stand-up guys willing to re-up with Uncle Sam for one last mission …with one exception—the son of a bitch who wound up with the money. A man who had been disfigured in the war and felt his government owed him in a big way. The man you heard confess, Kim. The man I shot on a windy runway in Nuevo Cadiz."

Kim had nodded all through that, but now she held my eyes with so much concern in hers, I knew something bad was coming.

She said, "I agree with your high assessment of the character of your old war buddies…with that one notable exception. But Morgan…I'm sorry to have to tell you this…your friend, Art Keefer—last surviving member of your original Army heist crew—was killed last month."

"Shit," I said. I felt like I'd taken a body blow. "How?"

Art had helped us with surreptitious transport on the Nuevo Cadiz mission, but I'd stayed out of contact with him since, for his own protection—or anyway, what I'd thought was his own protection.

"A plane crash," she said. "He was a pilot—what better way? Pilot error, they say, flying one of his small aircraft."

"In a pig's ass," I said.

"You said Art wasn't in on that forty-million haul, Morgan …but are you *sure*?"

"I guess under the circumstances, I can't be. Maybe that's why Art helped me out when he shouldn't have risked it— maybe he felt bad that I wound up blamed for a score I had nothing to do with."

"But a score somebody signed your name to," Kim said. "What about the other two on your crew?"

"Deceased. You know that."

"Just in the last couple of years, right? Again, well after the money-truck heist? Meaning everybody on your crew but you, Morg, is dead now."

I frowned, thinking it through. "One died of cancer, the other in an automobile accident—I never considered their deaths might have been liquidations."

She cocked her head, raised an eyebrow. "The Company has given more people cancer than Phillip Morris. And do I have to tell you that a car crash can be staged?"

I shook my head. "Damn. I should have *seen* that. *Damn!*"

"Don't beat yourself up—until Keefer's convenient death, I didn't put it together, either."

She stroked my cheek. Kissed me with a tenderness that made my heart ache almost as much as something else was aching.

"Darling," she said, "we've both been working on this, from our respective positions. I know what you've been doing, all these months. Besides keeping your head down, you've been moving from coastal city to coastal city, going to museums and rare book stores and university libraries, tracking your namesake...."

"Sir Henry Morgan," I said, nodding. "Before I shot my old buddy in the head, back in Nuevo Cadiz, he said he'd hidden the forty mil where Sir Henry kept *his* treasure. I figure the original Morgan's treasure is long gone, but my old pal found one of the treasure hideaways and buried the loot. I have half a dozen good leads to track down between Panama and Jamaica."

"Find that money," she said, "and turn it in, and with my testimony to back you up, you're a free man again. No more federal hounds on your trail."

"Right."

"But, darling, don't you see, there's *another* way...expose the government traitor who set you up! And I believe the name of that traitor can be found, right here in Miami."

I squinted at her, as if I were trying to bring that lovely face into sharper focus. "You said you were deep cover. What are you doing in Miami?"

"You and I are after the same prey—Jaimie Halaquez, the man who raided the treasury of the Cuban exiles here."

"I thought the CIA was out of the Cuba business."

"Overtly we are. Even covertly, not so much now. But these people were our allies, *are* our allies, and we keep an eye on them, their activities, and those who move against them. And they have something in common with the Company that I work for—they, too, have a traitor in their midst."

"Halaquez," I said.

"No," she said, and shook her head firmly. "Halaquez is just a henchman for a traitor still among them. But if we can *find* Halaquez, and make him talk…and we *can* make him talk, Morgan…he will lead us to the one he's working for. The one who has seen to it that for the last several years, all of the efforts of Little Havana's Cuban exiles have gone for nothing."

I laughed without humor. "I had that bastard in my damn hands, but he slipped out of them."

"Halaquez?"

"Yes," I said, and filled her in on my side of things.

It took a good ten minutes, going through in a linear fashion, starting with Pedro and company recruiting me to recover the stolen seventy-five grand, and winding up with the beating of Tango in her motel room, with me killing Halaquez's crony there and Halaquez himself getting away.

"This has to be about more than just the seventy-five thousand dollars," she said, when I finished, her expression and tone intense. "Two Cuban heavies, imported to back Halaquez up? It has to be much more."

"The answer," I said, "is tied up with this Richard Best character."

"Him I've never heard of," she admitted. "That's a new lead...and maybe you *should* keep chasing it down." She took my face in her hands and said, "We're very close. You keep up your efforts on the Best front. Can I contact you here?"

"Yes, through the madam—Bunny."

She nodded. "I know Bunny. This house is an intelligence resource for the Company. Morg, you can reach me at the Raleigh Hotel. I'm registered as Kim Winters."

That made me smile—Winters was the name I'd married her under, using "Morgan" as a first name.

"Spies shouldn't be sentimental slobs," I told her.

Her smile turned up wickedly at one corner. "I never said I was perfect, did I?"

"No. That was me who said that about you."

She gave me a kiss, nothing hot, just friendly, and slid off the bed.

"Gotta go," she said.

I followed her to the hidden door. "Why? Look, that bed is as good as any other. We've talked our business. So let's get *down* to business."

She shook her head. "I would like nothing better than to crawl under those covers with you and not come out for a week. But we don't *have* a week, and I'm just stubborn enough to want to start this marriage off with better than a quickie."

"Aw, Kim, for Christ's sake...."

"Morg, do you know who I report to? Do you know who's in town, running the Halaquez operation? Or did your ego tell you *you* were the star of the show?"

My mouth dropped and the words crawled out. "Not... Crowley."

"Yes. Your own personal Inspector Gerard himself. I report directly to him, and he knows about us, so he's been watching me like a hawk. That's why I've waited for days to risk this. My love...we *must* be careful."

I took her by the arms, firm, almost rough. Almost. "I want to see him."

"What?"

"Crowley. Goddamnit, Kim, we're working on the same case. I want Halaquez, and so, apparently, does he. I want a chance to sit down with him at a neutral place, and see if we can't come up with a truce till this thing is over."

"Morgan, I don't really think that's—"

"Kim, I am trying to conduct an investigation, a manhunt, from a goddamn whorehouse bedroom. I have something in common with the Cubans—I want some freedom. What do you say?"

Her eyes were slitted with worry. "If he knows we've had contact, I would be in a shitload of trouble."

"Then make up a story. Say I tracked you down, and we talked just long enough for me to make this request."

She thought about it.

Then she nodded, crisply. "All right. Is there a phone in here?"

"No, but Bunny has one."

Bunny—who was learning not to ask too many questions— gave us the use of both her office and her phone.

Kim dialed the Raleigh, said, "Room 414, please," and moments later had Crowley on the line, telling him she was sitting in an all-night diner near the City Curb Market, and that I'd come out of nowhere and braced her.

"Crowley wants to talk to you," she said, putting just the right alarm and hesitancy in her voice.

She gave me the receiver.

"Hi, Walter. Long time no see."

"Morgan," Crowley said, giving it the inflection of a curse. "I guess I should have kept a tail on that wife of yours."

"She's not my wife. That was just a cover story, old buddy. I want a few minutes of your time. We have some mutual interests here in Miami that could be served."

"...All right. You'll want the meet in a neutral place."

"Tomorrow morning, ten o'clock, Bayfront Park. Find your- self a seat in that amphitheater, and come alone. Keep in mind what happened to Mayor Cermak in that arena."

"All right, Morgan. I'll keep that in mind. And I'll come alone."

"I see any sign of agents backing you up, no meet. Got it?"

"Got it."

I hung up.

Kim said, "He agreed to it?"

"Yeah."

"He'll have agents there, Morg."

"Oh, I know. They'll be hard to spot. They'll be the ass-holes in dark suits and ties."

That made her smile.

Then I walked her up to Gaita's room and, before I could convince her that another half an hour would be worth risking, my bride had flown.

The cab dropped me under the front awning of the Raleigh Hotel, a 1930s-modern hotel dating to the pre-war boom, when that ten-mile sandbar called Miami Beach really took off. In a black sport jacket, charcoal sport shirt, and gray trousers, I looked like just another fairly well-off tourist, though my only baggage was the .45 under my arm.

I didn't enter the lobby, instead skirting around the building to where a massive if oddly shaped swimming pool was alive with Latin-styled popular music, laughter, and splashing. A nice salty breeze was rolling in off the ocean, but it was still a warm night. Lots of pretty girls in bikinis sunning by Hawaiian-type torchlight were getting plied with mixed drinks by determined guys in bathing suits, who knew that at a little after one o'clock A.M., they better get lucky damn soon.

Avoiding the lobby probably hadn't been a necessity—I wasn't checking in, or even asking for information, so the desk having my photo probably didn't come into play. Though I supposed it was possible that *some* security was lounging in the lobby.

But I didn't think so. An advantage the hunted has over

the hunter is that the hunter is seldom in hiding. The hunter never thinks about getting stalked himself.

So when I knocked on the door of room 414, it only took two knocks before it cracked open, without even a "Who is it?" Which meant I'd wasted time coming up with the "Telegram, Mr. Crowley" gag.

I pushed the door open, grabbing Crowley by the arm with one hand—he was in a terrycloth Raleigh bathrobe over blue silk pajamas—and with the other whipping the .45 out, kicking the door closed behind me.

I dragged him into the hotel room—not a suite, just a good-size room with sea-foam coloration and modern furnishings, if 1937 was your idea of modern. I dumped him on the bed, went over and double-locked the door, using the night latch, commenting, "You ought to try this thing—it's the latest in security measures," then came back, pulled up a rounded pink chair that was more comfortable than it looked and sat across from him. Pointing the .45 at him in a not terribly menacing way.

Just menacing enough.

"Hello, Walter."

"You're out of your goddamn mind!" Crowley spat.

That bland mug of his actually worked up some emotion, the tiny dark eyes dancing with outrage in the pale oval face under the thinning amber hair. His fists were clenched, and they looked small, like a child's. He wasn't a small man, but he was smaller than me, and fish-belly pale.

Bureaucrats can make your life a living hell, but they often don't look like much in the flesh.

"I decided to move our meeting up a few hours," I said. "And change the location. Last-minute changes for meets, there's another security measure you Company boys may want to consider."

"Morgan, there are half a dozen agents on this floor!"

"Yeah, all snug in their beds, or maybe down by the pool trying to get laid. Guys on your side of the fence never figure they need any protection. You're big bad G-men, after all."

"What the hell do you want?"

"Like I said on the phone—I want to talk. I just don't want to get my ass hauled off to the slammer before we have the chance to confab."

"I told you I'd come alone tomorrow."

"Yeah, well, you were lying. But I don't hold that against you. I already knew I wasn't going to show up at that park."

His upper lip curled back in outrage, exposing too much gum and tiny white teeth. "*Where* is Kim Stacy? What have you *done* with Kim Stacy!"

"I left her in that diner. She's probably back in her room, by now, down the hall, if you're to be believed. Why don't you call her? But she might be cross, if you wake her up."

His eyes tightened. "She doesn't have anything to do with this?"

"No. But I did talk to her, and she did admit that you people are looking for Jaimie Halaquez, too."

His eyes stayed tight and his chin crinkled. *Should he talk to me?* Finally he decided. "That's right, Morgan. We are."

I grinned at him. "You weren't in Miami looking for me. You were already here on the Halaquez case. And I just walked into it."

Crowley nodded. "But I think we gave you proper attention. I don't think you need to feel neglected."

"No, no complaints. You've kept me hopping. It's tempting just to shoot you, so I can hijack that bed for a decent night's sleep."

He smiled a little. It bordered on a sneer. "But you're not a killer, Morgan. You kill, but only in self-defense."

"Well, Walter, I'd guess I'd have to agree with you. But that's more a rule of thumb than a rule. You still don't want to get on my bad side."

"I would guess I already am."

"Not really. You're just a guy trying to do your job. You're a working stiff who's confused and doesn't know it, because you're on the wrong track. I'm not the guy you should be going after."

That got half a smile out of him, putting a dimple in that smooth face. "Really? Who *is* the guy I should looking for?"

"Hell, I don't know. All I know is, I didn't take down that money truck. Kim Stacy told you what she heard on that runway in Nuevo Cadiz, didn't she?"

"She did. But we discounted it. You have a reputation for having a certain…charm. Especially with the ladies."

"And yet you kept her on the company payroll? Didn't discipline her in any way?"

Crowley's tone was gently mocking. "Why should a woman be disciplined for loyalty to her own husband? Besides, she's a fine agent."

"Sure, Walter. And there's that other little thing."

"What other little thing is that, Morgan?"

"That someday she might lead you to me."

"And here you sit."

"And there *you* sit. While here I sit with a gun."

"You won't use it."

"Don't push it, Walter. Look, I don't expect you not to do your job. But since you didn't come to Miami looking for me—since Jaimie Halaquez was the man you were after—why don't you just postpone the Morgan manhunt until the other job is done?"

"Why should I do that?"

"Because I'm looking for Halaquez, too. I'm working on behalf of the Cuban exiles he robbed. I want to get their money back for them. And I'd be glad to turn him over to you when I've shaken that dough out of him."

He laughed. A small laugh, but a laugh. "You think you'll get him before we do? We have an operation already well underway."

"Well, I have my charm, remember. It's possible, going down my own paths and byways, that I might get to him before you do. My priority is that money."

He stopped smiling. He was thinking.

Finally, cocking his head, he said "What are you proposing?"

"Not that we throw in together, not exactly. Just call off the dogs. Let me move freely through this city. I'll keep you informed, calling you here at the hotel. And if I find him, and don't have to kill him...he's yours."

Crowley's eyes moved with thought as he tried to find a flaw in my proposal.

Then he asked, "And what then?"

"After I turn him over…or after you catch him, if I'm not part of it…you pay me the courtesy of giving me twenty-four hours before you open the Company kennels again. It's a fair request, Walter."

"It's fair, but it's nothing my superiors would endorse."

"Don't ask them. Someday I'll prove my innocence, and you'll know you did the right thing."

Crowley thought some more.

Then: "*Oh*-kay….but there's nothing I can give you but my word."

"I accept that."

He laughed, loud enough to ring off the plaster walls. "Are you sure? You didn't believe me on the phone when I said I'd come alone tomorrow."

"We're in the same room, and we're looking at each other. And you're looking down the barrel of my gun. I'll take your word."

He nodded. "What now?"

"I've already briefed Kim Stacy on my activities of the last few days. She can fill you in."

And that would leave how much she told Crowley to her own discretion.

I went on: "But with one of the byways I'm going down, I could use some help."

"You said we wouldn't be working together."

"This is just some information that I could use. You may not even have it."

"All right. Go ahead, Morgan. Ask."

"Does the name Richard Best mean anything to you?"

"No."

"How about Richard Parvain?"

Now he frowned. "*Parvain* you say? You wouldn't be talking about an inventor by any chance?"

"That's right. What's the story on him?"

His eyebrows went up, stayed there a few seconds, then came down again. "Well, he never worked for the government, not as an employee. Always on contract. I can't tell you *what* he was working on—"

"I can tell you. He was developing a sort of Geiger counter that could make its readings from a great distance. Like in an airplane."

His eyebrows went up and down again, more quickly this time. "All right. I won't deny that. The device was helpful. But then Parvain had a nervous breakdown, and a drinking problem, and he became a bad risk. He had another, even more important concept that he never delivered on. Finally, ties were cut with him."

"How long ago?"

"Oh…five years…seven years."

"What was the 'important concept'?"

"Morgan, that's classified—you know I can't…"

"Crowley, you said yourself Parvain never delivered. What was the concept?"

"Why?"

"Because he was murdered two days ago. Under the Richard Best name."

Crowley's eyes widened. "Christ. What were the circumstances?"

I told him.

Then I said, "What was the invention he promised but couldn't come through on?"

Crowley's sigh seemed to come from his toes. "It was an extension, an expansion of his original idea. This was a device that could detect the presence of atomic materials on the ground...from the air."

"You mean—a spy plane could know if an enemy had a storehouse of nuclear materials? Could pinpoint the location of missiles in silos? Could—"

He raised his hand. "Those applications and many more. When Parvain began his work on the project, we were especially sensitive to the threat of nuclear warheads in Cuba—it was a way to make sure the Russians hadn't secretly outfitted Cuba with missiles."

I let out a low whistle.

With a weary shrug, the man in the bathrobe said, "The government put a lot of money into the project, but finally pulled the plug. Parvain insisted on working alone, without supervision. He was, frankly, a crank. And then a crazy crank, and finally an alcoholic one. Morgan, you don't seriously believe he *did* finalize those plans?"

Now it was my turn to sigh from my shoes. I rose. I put the .45 away.

"Walter, if a scientist being crazy or a boozer precluded his ability to come up with innovations, you and I would be going to work every day in a horse and buggy."

And I left him there to think that over.

That and the rest of it.

CHAPTER ELEVEN

There's an old Army dodge that anyone carrying a clipboard stacked with printed forms, a pocketful of yellow pencils, and one of those inspection team expressions was a guy to stay away from. In a hospital, just add a white lab-type coat, and watch everybody you pass get suddenly too busy to talk, finding only enough time to smile politely and scurry away on unknown business.

Watch out for the man with clipboard, people! What you don't tell him, he can't write down....

So there was no trouble getting to the right floor and the right room at Miami General. The police guard on the door was a sleepy-eyed kid of maybe twenty-three sitting on a folding chair. His head was down and he might have been napping when I approached and cleared my throat. His eyes popped open and his chin jutted upward.

In my most officious tone, I asked, "Has any unauthorized party tried to get in to see Miss Prosser?"

"N-no, sir," he said, and began to get up.

I motioned for him to stay put. "Has she had *any* visitors this morning?"

"Just Sgt. Patterson of Homicide and Lt. Davis from Burglary. You're, uh, with the hospital, sir?"

I glared at him. "You're just getting around to asking me that?"

And I shook my head disgustedly and went into Tango's room, shutting the door on the young cop's sputtered apology.

Her eyes were closed. Possibly she was asleep, but in any case, breathing regularly, hooked up on an I.V., the shapely slenderness of her tall frame obvious under the sheet. Even battered and swollen and bandaged, her face held the striking exotic beauty that had allowed her to get out of her drunken father's house—of course, she'd only traded it for a brothel, but still an improvement. Her bed was cranked up somewhat, and her arms weren't under the covers, her dark tan a stark contrast with the hospital gown and sheets.

As I approached the bed, her eyes half opened. "Doctor…?"

"No," I said. "My name's Morgan."

Her eyes opened all the way, not quite startled, big dark brown pools. This was a lovely woman, all right, even after that bastard Halaquez had got through with her.

"You're Bunny's friend," she said.

"Yes." I gestured to the white lab coat, and tossed the clipboard onto her bedside table next to the water and Kleenex box. "This is just a get-up to avoid too many questions, coming to see you. How you doing, kid?"

She smiled. "I have a little button I can press when I want more morphine."

Her mouth, even without lipstick, provided a wide, attractive frame for perfect teeth that must have come from God, because her old man surely hadn't paid many dental bills.

"You been pushing the happy button much?"

Her laugh was just a little punch of air. "Now and then. I'm doing all right. Nothing was broken. But that Jaimie…

he, uh…really knows how to hurt a girl's feelings, huh?"

I leaned in. Spoke softly. "You prefer Tango or Theresa?"

"I feel more like Theresa right now."

"Okay, Theresa. Did they tell you that Halaquez got away, but that his helper didn't? That the helper got killed in a struggle there in your motel room?"

She nodded.

"Don't spread it around," I said, and risked a smile, "but I'm the guy who cluttered your room up with that trash. I wish I'd gotten there sooner. And your friend Jaimie slipped through my damn fingers, I'm not proud to say."

"Jaimie was…was never my friend. I knew him from the Mandor, a little. I heard about him from other girls. I don't go that route."

"What route?"

"The bondage route. That's Jaimie's thing, you know. He wants to be hurt. Then later…he wants to hurt *you*. That's what I hear, anyway, from my co-workers. He, uh…really does seem to know his way around torture."

"Then why did you have his picture? It was in one of your purses in your room at the club."

"Dickie gave that to me."

"Dickie. Dick Best?"

She nodded. "He gave me that picture and said that if anything ever happened to him, give it to the police. I took it and said I would, but never did, or…haven't yet. When I heard Dickie was dead, I was sorry…I cried. But I didn't want to get involved any more than I already was."

"But you recognized the picture."

"Yes, only I didn't tell Dickie. He might have misunderstood if he thought I knew Jaimie. Might've thought I'd been one of Jaimie's girls at the Mandor, even though I wasn't. You see, Dickie...he was different. He was...special."

"How so, Theresa?"

"He was an older man, you know...he only wanted to protect me. Wanted me to go off with him and...and we would start over somewhere. Dickie was a very smart man. He was an inventor...."

"I know. Theresa, I have to ask this. You don't really like men, do you? I have an idea you like women better."

Her smile was a tiny white thing in the beautiful battered face. "I don't like sex at all, Mr. Morgan."

"Just 'Morgan.' Then why would you go into the sex-for-money trade?"

"Because it's just that. A trade. I am a good-looking woman, or anyway I am when I'm not covered in bruises and burns. My looks, Morgan...they're really all I've got. I'm not stupid, but I'm not smart." The exotic face took on a sudden hard cast. "I'm a good-looking piece of ass, and so that's the commodity I sell."

"Is that how Dickie Best looked at you? As a good-looking piece of ass?"

Her smile disappeared. Her eyes moistened. "No. He said I was his...his poor little lost lamb."

"Your relationship wasn't sexual?"

"Not...not mostly sexual. Dickie, he...oh, he *liked* sex. We had sex sometimes. Mostly I just...I just used my hand. That seemed enough. He was more a friend to me. Someone I admired. Someone who was kind. Someone who loved me, but didn't force me to do anything I didn't want to."

The decent father she never had, if you factored out the hand jobs.

"We were going to go off together," she said. "Dickie said he already had a...his words were, 'Decent amount of money.' But he could get more. He said he thought he could...I don't know exactly what this means, Morgan, but this is what he said...he said, 'I think I can shake half a million out of them. Then we can go to Mexico and live like royalty.' He said it was cheap to live in Mexico."

"Do you have any idea who it was he planned to shake that money out of?"

"It must have been Jaimie Halaquez. Otherwise, why would Dickie leave me that picture? And why would Jaimie come to my motel room and...and do what he did?"

"What did Jaimie want from you?"

"He wanted to know everything that Dickie had said. I told him. I didn't tell him about the photo because I thought that might get me killed. But I told him everything else. Only...that wasn't enough. Jaimie was convinced that I *had* something, something *valuable*, something that Dickie had given me. But I didn't. I don't."

"What was that valuable thing?"

"I don't know!"

"When he worked you over, Theresa, didn't Halaquez say what he was looking for?"

"No! Just...'*Where is it?*' Over and over again...*where is it!*"

The door opened and I turned, wondering if I'd been made, hoping that if it was cops, Crowley calling off the dogs included alerting the local canines that I was off the federal wanted list.

But it wasn't a dog at all—it was a Bunny.

Funny to see her in a black-and-gray business suit, looking more like an officer at a bank than a whorehouse madam. Even all that blonde hair was pinned back in a dignified way, though there was no hiding the purple streaks.

"Morgan," Bunny said, and rushed to my side. "How's my girl doing?"

"Ask her yourself," I said, turned to smile and nod at the patient, then stepped aside.

I took a chair in the corner while the two women talked for about five minutes. Nothing touched upon why I was here. Finally I called Bunny over and she pulled a chair around, so we were facing each other. I saw Theresa thumb her morphine button, and her eyes closed, and she drifted off early in my conversation with Bunny, which was whispered.

"You're taking a chance, being here," Bunny said to me.

"Not as big as it used to be. I've worked out a truce with that fed, Crowley, though I'm not sure the white flag extends to the local fuzz."

"I can spread that word to my contacts on the Miami PD," Bunny said, "if it'll help."

"Worth a try. What do those cop contacts have to say about Tango's situation?"

"Nobody has any idea that Morgan the Raider was in that

motel room. They think another guest at the Vincalla heard the scuffle, got involved, and one of Tango's torturers got himself plugged with his own gun in the process. The fuzz figure this guest called it in and then made himself scarce."

"And that's as far as it goes?"

"No, they're investigating. Questioning the other motel guests."

"Good. That'll keep 'em busy. Did they say anything about the Best killing? I understand cops from both Homicide and Burglary were here talking to Tango this morning."

Her eyes and nostrils flared like a filly's on its hind legs. "Damn, Morgan—you pick up information like blue serge does lint. As it happens, there's an oddity about the Best killing that's come up. Seems two neighbors at Best's apartment house report hearing what might have been a scuffle next door, tallying with the approximate time of death."

"That's not surprising."

"No, but these neighbors also heard noises *later* on…not another scuffle, but sounds that could have been Best's room being tossed…that same night. About two hours after."

"Really? Interesting."

"Interesting? That all you have to say, Morg? What's it mean?"

It might mean Halaquez had killed Best prematurely, and whoever he reported to had sent Jaimie's dumb ass back to search for the same unknown item that Tango had been tortured over.

"No idea," I told her.

"Listen, there's something that may or may not mean a

damn thing. Gaita's kind of…well, fallen off the map."

"*What?*"

"Morgan—easy. I probably overstated it. She took off early yesterday, without saying anything, which is unusual. Today's her regular day off, but I don't get any answer where she stays, when she isn't at the Mandor."

"I should check this."

She held up a hand. "I already did. I stopped by on my way here. Her landlady was there and said Gaita hasn't been around for several days. I asked to look in her room, but she wasn't there."

"Any sign of a struggle? Anything unusual?"

"No. Sometimes that girl just takes off, to be by herself. The only thing really unusual is, well…with what's going on lately, I would think she would stick around. In case she was needed."

"Did you check with her friends in Little Havana? Pedro and Maria…?"

"Yes. They haven't heard from her either. Really, it's probably nothing. Hasn't even been twenty-four hours. But I figured you should know."

I nodded, troubled but not sure if I needed to be, and not knowing what the hell I could do about it, if I did need to be.

Theresa was asleep as I headed out, so when Bunny called to stop me, her voice was hushed: "*Oh*—Morgan. Something else…."

I went over to her. She was getting in her purse.

"This came today," she said, and handed me an opened

envelope. It was addressed to Bunny at the Mandor Club, no return address, and inside was a kid's birthday card with bunnies on it.

Tucked in the card was a thousand dollars in C-notes.

No signature.

"Best?" I said.

She shrugged and nodded at the same time. "I think it's that late birthday present he promised me. Must have been forwarded by a lawyer or something."

"Was there anything else in the envelope?"

"Yes...but not addressed to me."

She got back in her purse and found a tiny manila envelope that said: *Please give to Tango for me. R.B.*

My fingers told me it was a key.

"I'm taking this," I said.

She didn't argue. "What is it?"

I tore open the envelope, shook the contents into my palm, showed her the key there. It said *UBS 117.*

Glancing over at the battered beauty, I said, "I think it's what Tango got the hell beat out of her over."

I gave the startled-looking Bunny a kiss on the cheek, slipped the key back in its little envelope, and dropped it in my sportcoat pocket.

On the way out I told the young cop at the door to stay sharp.

"Somebody may to try to kill that woman," I told him, jerking a thumb at the hospital room door.

His eyes popped. "You really think so?"

"A possibility. One other thing."

"Yeah?"

"Start checking I.D."

He was nodding at the wisdom of that as I walked away.

The Union Bus Station on Northeast First Street was fairly dead just after lunch. I was all alone at the wall of lockers when I searched out number 117, tried the key, and found nestled within a black leather bag that resembled the sort of bag doctors carried, back when house calls were more common.

I admit to being surprised—I figured on finding an envelope, a much larger manila one than the little key had come in. Surely what Halaquez and his boss were after were the finished plans to that improved version of Best's atomic divining rod.

How else could the crackpot inventor have expected to come up with the kind of loot he'd told Tango he could "shake out of them"?

I wandered into the men's room. There were half a dozen sinks and as many stalls, but right now I had the place to myself. Taking no chances, I selected a stall, faced the toilet, put a foot on the stool, and propped the Gladstone bag against my leg—no lock on the thing, it just popped right open....

The money was stacked in there with a scientist's precision. It was all kinds of bills, mostly small and well-used, and I wasn't about to take the time and trouble to count it; but odds were this was the bulk of the seventy-five grand that my Little Havana employers had asked me to recover.

It should be at least $1000 short, because Bunny had

earned her late birthday present for being the buffer between Tango and the hidden loot.

And now I got it.

Now it made sense, everything falling into place like the tumblers of a lock picked by an expert safecracker.

Dick Best recognizes Jaimie Halaquez at the Mandor Club from back when both were working with the CIA on various Cuba libre projects. The aging inventor approaches Halaquez and tells the Cuban that he's developing an atomic-materials detector, a potentially key discovery in the Cold War arms race.

Halaquez steals $75,000 from the Cuban exiles' treasury and funds Best's research project. In the meantime, Halaquez goes into hiding, moving from one safe house in one city to another in another, until finally returning to Miami to collect on his investment.

But for reasons unknown, Best does not or cannot deliver—possibly the inventor had been scamming his angel all along, or likely Best demanded more money, saying additional research was required.

Either way, Halaquez decides to cut his losses, and the only further payment Best gets is a fatal karate chop to the back of the neck.

But when Halaquez reports in, his superior sends his heavy-handed minion back to Best's apartment to search it—for either the atomic plans, the money…or both.

Torturing Tango was likely an attempt to find those plans, not retrieve the relatively paltry seventy-five grand. But the importance of the invention Best was dangling in front of the Commies explained why heavies from Cuba had been imported to give Halaquez a hand....

This was speculation, of course, but informed speculation, and as if more proof were needed, the door to my stall was kicked open, swiping me across the back and sending me off balance, only to catch myself with a hand against the wall. I looked back and saw a guy a head taller than me with skin the color of coffee-with-cream—spiffy in a sharply cut brown suit with black lapels—grinning (he had a golden incisor) the way a big rapist does at a little girl.

Then he grabbed me by the shoulders and dragged me out of the stall and flung me against the row of sinks. The doctor's bag of money, which I hadn't snapped shut, stayed in the stall, clunking on its side on the tile floor, spilling cash.

I hit hard, but not so hard that I couldn't whip my .45 out from under my arm, only the big guy, who looked like a linebacker but had a ballet dancer's grace, nimbly kicked the gun from my hand, his pointy Cuban boot jabbing my right wrist. The automatic skittered and spun on the tile floor, way out of reach. He was coming at me with clawed hands outstretched and with a gold-toothed grin that seemed at once menacing and simple-minded, and I braced my hands on the edge of sink behind me, lifted myself and kicked out with both feet and caught him in the chest.

He went windmilling back, slapping open and returning to the stall he'd dragged me from, moisture catching his fancy boots and depositing him on the floor, the stool stopping him, and this time it was my attacker who was clawing for a rod under his arm, a .22 automatic that was aimed right at me when I was all but on top of him, and I batted it away and took him by the legs and upended him. He conked his head on the porcelain edge of the crapper, dazing himself, and then I lifted him up and over and dunked him in, so that he made a splashing underwater headstand in the bowl. I had him around the waist and I hugged him like I loved him, his feet kicking harmlessly above me, his hands trying to swim in the air but getting nowhere, swiping at me but seldom landing and then with more hysteria than power, and it took him probably two gurgling minutes to drown.

I pulled him up and out and sat him loosely on the stool. His eyes were open but not seeing anything, and his hair, which had been slicked back like George Raft's, was trailing down his forehead in damp seaweed tendrils now. I had gotten pretty wet myself, my pants anyway, and I was exhausted. You try holding a two-hundred-pound bastard upside down in a john and see if you don't come out wiped.

When I shut him in there, all you could see were two feet visible under the door of a stall. The floor was a little water-pooled in there, but otherwise it was normal enough a sight.

I retrieved my .45 and stuck it back under my arm.

At the row of sinks, I repacked the Gladstone bag, some of the bills pretty damp. With the party over, I was more attuned to the danger of somebody coming in on me, but either nobody at the bus station had time to go before catching their ride, or I was even luckier than usual.

I even took time to throw some water on my face and stand there till my breathing was back to normal. I looked at myself in the mirror and answered my own unasked question.

He must have been watching the hospital, spotted me, and followed me here. Whoever he was.

But I *knew*, didn't I? This was the third Castro Cuban I'd killed in two days....

On the way out, I understood why we hadn't been disturbed—my assailant had thoughtfully hung an OUT OF ORDER sign on the door. I guessed I owed him one, but didn't feel too bad I'd never get the chance to repay him.

The diner I was meeting Muddy Harris at was only half a dozen blocks from the bus station, so I walked it, and the Miami sunshine dried my trousers by the time I got there. I spotted the bail bondsman in a back booth, waved at him, he waved back, but first I needed the men's room.

For a less strenuous session, I hoped.

It was a one-seater with a single urinal, and you could lock the door, which I did. At the sink, I unloaded the bag of money, and did a fast but probably accurate count.

There was one-hundred-and-twenty grand in the bag. So Best had squeezed that $75,000 out of Halaquez, and a little more. That gave me an extra $45,000 to play with. If I were a great guy, I would hand that over to the Cuban exiles, too. But I was Morgan the Raider, who just drowned a guy in a toilet, so I would pocket the excess for my trouble.

That Muddy was having a piece of pie did not surprise me. That he could eat that way, and carry all that weight around, and still find clothes that looked baggy on him, remained a mystery.

"I hear the heat's off," he said cheerfully.

"Temporarily," I said. "I struck a deal with Crowley."

"Do you trust him?"

"We have mutual interests. He's after Jaimie Halaquez, too. What is that, coconut cream? À la mode? Are you kidding?"

His frown was disgusted and disgusting, white-smeared as it was. "Do I look like I need health tips from Morgan the Raider? Listen, I can assure you the Mob is no part of what's been going down."

"You can, huh?"

He nodded, licked ice cream from his upper lip. "The Mob boys have really distanced themselves from the Cuban exile crowd, the last couple years. Not to mention the CIA—they feel they got burned. Anyway, it's looking obvious the casinos aren't going back in, in Havana, any time soon. And you were right—Castro's made a deal with Trafficante, and dope is flowing. Big heroin source."

"Which means...the Mob isn't part of this."

"Yeah, didn't I say that? But that's not the big news."

"Do I have to buy you more pie before you spill it?"

"Naw. I'm just having the one piece...that bring-your-own-whips-and-chains party on Palm Beach? At that rented mansion? It happens tonight."

I sat forward. "You know this how?"

"I have ops staking out the area, like you requested. They have this very day seen hookers streaming into that joint like ants to a picnic. These are not your run-of-the-mill chippies—real beautiful pieces, and word is, they are specialists. Domination. Bondage. The whole ball-gag bit."

"Coming from out of town, you think?"

"Oh, no question—some, anyway. There aren't that many of this specialized type of sex worker in Miami."

"And the Consummata herself?"

He shrugged, patting his comb-over in place. "Well, we don't know for a fact that this is the Consummata, Morgan. It just fits her M.O., is all. And how would I know her if I saw her? Other than she's a well-preserved old broad, by all accounts. I mean, she wears a leather mask and the whole nine yards. You know, the Lone Ranger or Zorro, they got nothing on her, and they don't have tits."

"What if I wanted a blueprint on this mansion?"

He didn't bother hiding his smugness. Both his grin and tone conveyed it. "I'm ahead of you, Morgan…but it'll cost you a thousand."

"What do I get for it?"

"How about floor plans? Also, the position of the dock off the back lawn, if you should want to show up by boat."

"Done."

The fleshy face creased in a smile and he pushed the cleaned plate aside, just as the waitress was coming by. She snagged it but Muddy stopped her, touching her arm. "Do that again, sweetheart, would you? But hold the ice cream. I'm watching my figure."

"Bring me a Key Lime," I said, smiling at her. She was a cute kid. "And some unsweetened iced tea."

I'd worked up an appetite.

"And sweetheart?" Muddy said to her back. She glanced over her shoulder. "Give my friend the check, would you?"

CHAPTER TWELVE

From a phone booth outside a gas station, I tried to get Kim at her room at the Raleigh. She didn't answer, but I did catch Crowley in his.

He said, "Was that your handiwork at the bus station?"

"It was self-defense."

"How do you drown somebody in self-defense?"

"Well, you have to be willing to get wet. Prick shouldn't have interrupted me in that stall. Whatever happened to common courtesy?"

"Jesus, Morgan. I give you a free pass and you—"

"What do the cops know?"

"Nothing to speak of. I haven't seen the body yet, but judging by the description, I'm thinking it's another of these hardcases imported from Cuba. I'm pretty sure we'll come up bupkus on prints."

"Yeah, I sincerely doubt he had a green card."

Crowley grunted. "Something a lot more important than a seventy-five grand score brings *that* kind of talent to town."

"No argument. I recovered the seventy-five thousand, by the way."

"*How?*"

"Not important. Let's just say, I found what those tourists from Havana were looking for. Any objection to my turning those greenbacks back over to the Cuban exiles?"

"If I had any objections, would it do any good?"

"No."

"Well…you have my blessing, anyway. More power to them. We weren't looking to recover that money as much as Halaquez himself. He could be a major source of information, under the right interrogation techniques."

"You better find him before I do."

"Morgan, you've done *enough* killing…."

"I'm not going to kill the bastard."

"No?"

"No. I'm just going to turn him in to the people he screwed over. Maybe they'll have some ideas of their own."

"Morgan—"

I hung up.

Once again, a taxi took me to Little Havana. By sunlight, it was a different place, with only the familiar coffee and tobacco scents to say otherwise. The Spanish architecture of Calle Ocho, its sidewalks shaded by nicely spaced palms, made an authentic backdrop to the outdoor cafes, gift shops and magic-potion dens courting tourists.

I was in a tan suit with a brown sport shirt and Ray-Bans, just another *gringo* rubbernecker. Only this *gringo* had a .45 under his arm and a money bag in his fist.

I'd called ahead, and soon I was sitting at the familiar dining table in the simple room of second-hand furnishings and Catholic icons in the living quarters over that grocery. Pedro, in a yellow pleated button-down shirt, had a matching cap before him on the table, like a dish he was preparing to eat. Next to him, dignified Luis Saladar—his plantation-owner white hat on the table—wore a cream-color suit with yet another black bolo tie.

Both men were smiling, but especially Pedro, his upraised grin at odds with his down-tipped *bandito* mustache.

No food was being served at this table—Maria wasn't with us this afternoon, working downstairs in the *tiendo*—but a feast had been served up. By me. I had dumped the black leather bag onto the table and turned Richard Best's neat stacks into an ungainly pile of money, all sorts of denominations, though rarely over $20, representing hundreds of small but hard-earned contributions from the Cuban exile community.

"That's seventy-five thousand," I said, "on the nose."

Saladar's smile became a curious frown. "Halaquez had not turned it into foreign currency, as you had thought?"

"No. No need. He was using it to fund a project here in the States."

"What project, *señor?*"

"Not important. What *is* important is that pile of cash."

Pedro, so happy his eyes brimmed with tears, said, "But you did not take out *your* payment, *Señor* Morgan! Do we not owe you another six-thousand-and—"

I held up a hand. "The five-thousand-dollar down payment will cover it, and my expenses. I recovered more money than this…" I nodded toward the cash "…and I've helped myself to the excess."

Saladar was really frowning now. "How *much* more, *señor?*"

"Does that matter? I fulfilled my contract at a bargain rate."

Pedro didn't care about such trivialities, though the exile leader remained troubled.

"I don't know where Halaquez got the extra dough," I said, answering the question in Saladar's eyes. "I will say he was working on something bigger than raiding your treasury. Three *asesinos* from Castro's Cuba have been backing him up, of late. I've taken out all three."

Pedro's smile finally vanished and he raised his hands as if in surrender. "Perhaps it is best you do not share all of this *informacion* with us, *señor*. We are very satisfied with these results. We do not...begrudge, is that the word? We do not begrudge you making a profit from your hard and most dangerous work."

"You're only disappointed," I said, reading it in his voice, "that I haven't killed Halaquez, or better still turned his sorry ass over to you."

"*Señor....*"

"Well, me, too, Pedro. But before I move on...and soon I'll have to, because the *federales* will come down on me before long...I have one last chance to catch this *bastardo*, Halaquez."

Still troubled, Saladar asked, "Would this require further payment, *Señor* Morgan?"

"No. This is something I can do toward that extra money I recovered. Plus, three times this son of a bitch has tried to have me killed. And who's to say he won't stay at it?"

Pedro said, "What can we do to help, *amigo*?"

"I need a boat. A cruiser, if possible. Something I can arrive in quickly, and leave the same way, with room for a passenger or two."

Saladar had lost his frown, and was thinking about smiling again. "A passenger like Jaimie Halaquez?"

"You got it. And I may need to keep it."

"Keep the boat, *señor*?"

"It may become my getaway ride from this part of the world. If I *do* keep it, I'll pay the freight, but you might have to wait for the money till I'm somewhere I can properly get it to you."

Pedro looked pointedly at Saladar. "What about *your* boat, Luis?"

That Saladar had access to a boat did not surprise me—the Cuban exiles would have any number of uses for one.

Saladar was already nodding. "I was thinking the same. *Señor* Morgan, I have the Chris-Craft. It is thirty-three feet. Two V8 engines. Would that do?"

I grinned at him, nodding. "That would do fine. It's your boat, you say?"

"*Si, señor*."

"What value would you place on it?"

"It is hard to say. It is several years old. Perhaps ten years. Still, it would be a considerable cost to replace it. And we would, *señor*, need to get another."

"How considerable?"

"I would say…fifteen thousand American?"

"All right. I may not have to hang onto it. That's just one of a number of things that I won't know until the time comes."

Saladar sat forward. "Do you need someone to watch your back, *amigo*?"

"Luis, I would hate to impose on your generosity yet again...."

He made a bowing gesture like a Middle Eastern pasha. "To accompany you would be an honor, *señor*. I will bring a gun, no?"

"You will bring a gun," I said, "yes."

The night was as clear and warmly windy as you might imagine of Miami, though under a sickle slice of moon, Biscayne Bay seemed uncommonly dark, with more light from the shorelines than the sky. And *shorelines* was right, because there were assorted islands to navigate, some—like Palm Island—man-made.

I sat with Saladar up on the flybridge of the Chris-Craft Futura, letting him play captain—these were his waters, after all, smooth waters right now, with only a gentle refreshing spray to remind us where we were.

We'd started out in a marina near Bayfront Park and cut between islands and under the MacArthur Causeway, which ran parallel to the ten-mile-wide Palm Island, coming up on the dockside down behind the old stucco mansion.

The boat Saladar provided was a good one, a rare Sport Express model dating to '57, black hull with brown and white trim, rakish as hell, the words *Black Beauty* on its stern. The cabin below had built-in couches and tables, and a well-equipped galley, with forward sleeping quarters. Not a bad candidate for Morgan the Raider's new galleon.

Cutting a dashing figure with his well-trimmed mustache and spade beard, Saladar had at my request worn black, a cap in place of his plantation hat, his shirt another of those pleated button-down jobs, his pants sporting a gaucho flare, with a .38 long-barrel revolver low on his hip, gunfighter-style.

My suit was a sharp charcoal number I picked up in Miami Beach, though the coat was a size up to help disguise the shoulder sling with .45, and to give me easy access to the razor-sharp six-inch throwing knife in the sheath strapped to my left forearm. My shirt was black, my tie midnight blue— dark enough to blend into the night, but a look suitable for just another sleazy well-off guest.

When we tied up, ours was the only boat at the little dock —no surprise, since no one lived at the mansion right now. Rows of palms bordered a back yard big enough to build half a dozen tract homes on, and there was just enough moonlight to reveal that the swimming pool was empty, cracked, and dirty looking.

The abandoned pool was halfway between here and the mansion, its neo-Spanish structure typical of the 1920's real estate boom, a little landscaped rise putting the massive structure up on a pedestal it no longer quite deserved. In the meager moonlight, I couldn't tell whether the house was white or beige or yellow, though the tile roof appeared to be a shade of dark green.

"Just sit up in the flybridge," I advised Saladar.

Right now we were on the dock.

He frowned and cocked his head. "I will be out in the open, *Señor* Morgan."

"Yes, and there'll be security working this shindig. They may notice you. Be friendly and just say you are waiting for the senator."

"*What* senator, *señor*?"

"Any senator. That's all you'll have to say, most likely. If they get nasty, show them your gun, then tie them up with that green tape I gave you."

"*Si, señor.*"

I had a roll of duck tape in my jacket pocket, too—I'd learned in the military that you could fix anything from a gun to a jeep with that stuff, and it made excellent gags and bindings. No way to conceal *that* bulge…but a necessary tool tonight.

I hoped not to kill anybody on this mission—even Halaquez. This was, after all, just a party for perverts, who probably deserved a spanking but not to be shot. And why spank somebody who would only enjoy it, unless maybe it's a beautiful willing woman?

"If you hear gunshots," I advised the exile leader, "don't leave until you see people streaming your way…but, man, if I'm running out in front of 'em, hold up."

"*Si, señor.* Do you anticipate trouble?"

"I'm delivering it."

"…But I am to avoid…" He frowned, calling up a phrase I'd used earlier. "…avoid the deadly force."

"You got it, Luis. Good luck, *amigo.*"

"Good luck, my friend."

Gun still tucked under my arm, I hugged the line of palms at left, moving low and slow. The mission-style mansion had only a few lights on downstairs, but plenty burning on the upper floor. I didn't see anybody back here patrolling the grounds.

That is, not until I assumed a more normal gait and posture, moving past the empty swimming pool and walking up the concrete steps to a patio devoid of outdoor furniture. Around the mansion to my right came a burly young guy with a short military haircut. Like me, he was in a dark suit, though his was indifferently tailored, making no attempt to conceal the gun under the left armpit of his unbuttoned coat.

"Can I help you, sir?" he said, his voice a no-nonsense baritone. Like a lot of military types, he could frown at you without any wrinkling around the eyes.

"Good evening," I said, and walked right up to him. "I just stepped out for some air." I grinned. "Things were gettin' a little hairy in there, know what I mean?"

But he wasn't having any of the we're-just-a-couple-of-regular-guys routine.

"I'll have to see your invitation, sir."

"Sure," I said, and whipped the .45 out, slamming the barrel against the side of his head, catching the edge of his face, opening it up to bleed some. He went down on one side and was either out or damn near, so I risked hauling him by the feet over to some bushes before I removed and tossed away his gun (a Glock) then duck-taped his hands behind him, and his ankles. He was just coming around when I smeared the slab of tape across his mouth.

Then I knelt and whispered in his ear: "You might be able to get to your feet and waddle around like an asshole. But then my friend keeping watch back here would have to shoot you."

His eyes, which had bulged with indignation as he craned

back at me, turned wary—probably as close to fear as this apparent ex-Marine could feel—and his muttering beneath the duck-tape gag ceased.

"You just stay put, catch a little nap. You're going to have a scar on your face that the ladies will just love."

I would have left it at that, but the wariness of those eyes turned a nasty shade of cold, so I had to kick him in the head. It wouldn't kill him, I didn't think. But it did guarantee that nap I'd suggested.

I went up half a dozen cement steps onto a stoop, then in the unlocked back door into a good-size white '30s-modern kitchen—the only light on was over the sink. Despite the party underway, this was a kitchen empty of food or any preparation thereof, with the exception of an impressive array of liquor bottles on a counter—back-up supplies, perhaps, for various wet bars around the facilities.

Though I shut the door as silently as I could, another military-trained bouncer type came in from a hallway and asked, "May I help you, sir?"

"Just getting some air." I gave him a shaggy grin. "You need to see my invitation, I bet."

I left him in the otherwise empty pantry.

The downstairs and its many rooms of various sizes was vacant—no furniture, no people, a light on in the hall and on the stairs, but nowhere else. I moved through like a ghost haunting the dark, musty house, which wasn't rundown but really could stand renovation. Like the high ceilings with their vintage light fixtures, the walls were cracked here and there, with occasional nails and faded patches indicating where pictures had once hung, and the dark woodwork had seen better days. The floors were parquet and I was glad my shoes had rubber soles.

I took this tour uninterrupted—the guy who'd met me in the kitchen must have been working the front door, or perhaps somebody was standing outside, checking invitations. I didn't see the percentage in going out there. Funny, though, for the first floor of this big, grand, if out-of-date house to be such a hollow deserted shell, while the muffled yet distinct soundtrack of jazz bleeding down from upstairs told a different story...

...pulsing, discordant minor key music, unfamiliar to me, heavy on the sax and strip-club percussion, night music with a jungle beat and savage edge.

Just within the front door was a wide stairway that went up to a landing and took a left. I went up and on the landing almost ran into a plump barefoot near-naked bald man coming down. A nationally prominent Miami financier, he was wearing a diaper and a pink baby bonnet.

He nodded at me, said, "Nature calls," and went on his way.

This meant two things to me.

First, they served a variety of fetishes at this hullabaloo.

Second, since the baby man was unaccompanied, the downstairs (despite the lack of activity) was not off limits—the guests were free to come down to use the john. Fine. That indicated that—as long as I was perceived as just another guest—I wouldn't get much if any hassle upstairs....

Indeed I didn't. More security guys with guns under their dark suit coats were stationed in the hallway, off of which were half a dozen closed doors, behind which God knew what was transpiring. I counted four watchdogs, three that seemed to be maintaining their posts, and one who was strolling, just generally keeping an eye on things.

The latter stopped me, when I was about to head down the hallway to the right.

"Help you, sir?"

As it was, I knew right where I was going, thanks to the floor plan Muddy Harris had sold me. Plus, the muffled jungle jazz seemed to emanate from that direction, louder up here.

"Ballroom," I said, nodding in the direction I'd been heading.

I assumed the ballroom would be a more general entertainment area than the sealed-off bedrooms represented.

Right then, a guy exited one of the latter in a black leather vest and matching leather shorts and shiny-chained ankles that made him hop. He had a red ball gag in his mouth, like he was biting Bozo's nose, his hands cuffed behind him. A Latin gal in a redheaded wig and a black leather bikini with sheer black tights and very high heels was walking him along by a chain leash. They headed downstairs. I assumed, once there, she would thoughtfully help him use the head. He was, by the way, a nationally syndicated political columnist.

The watchdog said to me, "Ballroom? Double doors at the end of the hall."

I'd known that, but said, "Thanks, buddy."

I pushed through the double doors.

The music was almost deafening now, not a live combo, just jazz piped in via strategically positioned loudspeakers, a sax wailing above machine-gunning bongos while a thumping bass made rough love to itself. The combination of bright light and no light made my eyes go blurry for a while, but trying to focus on the spectacle before me would have been a challenge anyway. Cigar and cigarette smoke drifted like fog, and I had an idea maybe one of those dry-ice fog machines was adding to the weird, hazy atmosphere.

Here, bathed in red light, a bouffant blonde in a black corset and black stockings and garters and high heels was tying a redhead in a sheer green negligee to a tall sawhorse, the redhead's ankles spread and bound by cord to the rough wooden legs, wrists bound to the wood as well, body encased by an elaborately constricting leather harness with a padlock dangling at the crotch, her eyes wild, screaming silently behind a knotted gag.

What this ballroom had been in its day I had no idea, but right now it resembled nothing so much as a television studio, minus the cameramen. The walls were draped in black, and a lighting grid above sent its various beams crisscrossing through the big room to take aim at four platforms, one in each corner, where bondage tableaus were being staged.

There, drenched in blue lighting, a black-haired doll with Bettie Page bangs in a black bra and black latex toreador pants was tying a curly-headed brunette wearing sheer black bikini underthings to a prone metal tubular contraption that looked like a bizarre chiropractic table, the victim's eyes crazed above a red ball-gag, waist roped, wrists roped, ankles roped, to keep her legs wide spread.

These living pageants of pain were being performed for

men who either sat in comfortable leather chairs arranged as front-row seating or simply stood for a while and moved on to the next living display, like Stations of the Cross. There was no laughter, no yelling, no taunting or encouragement for the women performing, instead an almost church-like hushed awe came off the glazed, sometimes trembling spectators, prisoners of their obsessions, or perhaps wretched souls merely pummeled into silence by the bongo-driven, sax-screaming jazz.

Across the way, in a flickering strobe, two shapely young women in bra and panties and nylons with garters—one with French maid touches and both with the kind of spike heels that could put an eye out—were wrestling, each holding the other down, then wriggling free, and trading places in taking a prisoner.

These stages were perhaps three feet off the parquet dance floor, straddling the room's corners, the spotlights perfectly positioned, as no one was up there working them. This was a rehearsed show, well-practiced routines choreographed by a latter-day Marquis de Sade.

Opposite, in a green glow, an elaborate wooden rack with pulleys and ropes with straps held a saucer-eyed Asian beauty by the wide-spread wrists, while her face silently screamed with yet another ball-gag held in place by a head-hugging gizmo that might have come from a demented dentist, ankles held by other straps connecting to the elaborate rope set-up, and she wore nothing but black nylons and high heels, otherwise stark naked, while a German-looking pigtailed beauty in a black bra and panties and sheer black stockings and matching heels methodically went around pulling on and tightening the ropes.

Not my scene.

But I made the rounds anyway, moving from one tableau to another, until I fell in with a guy in a conservative brown suit who had a kind of State Fair demeanor. He was about forty, with a graying crew cut, and looked vaguely like Ozzie Nelson. He noticed me and I smiled, nodded, held up a hand for him to stop. He did.

"I got here late," I said, having to work to get heard over the blare of raunchy jazz. "What's the drill?"

"Your number's on the back of your invitation," he said.

"It is?"

"Yeah. When you hear it, just go over to the doors."

"And?"

His face burst into a goofball grin. "That's when you get your *private* party."

So this ballroom was just one big waiting room. A warm-up for the real deal. But just as I was thinking that I hadn't heard *any* numbers read, a sultry, throaty female voice cut in over the jazz on the loudspeakers: "*Number twelve. Number twelve.*"

My pal turned to me and his eyes went wide and he was beaming like Christmas. *That's me!* his stupid expression said.

And here I was without a number. Hell, without an invitation. *What was my next move?*

In making the rounds, I had already checked to see if Jaimie Halaquez was among the men waiting at this S & M Baskin Robbins. And there was no sign of him.

Maybe he was off in his private session. Or maybe he'd had it already and gone home, happily humiliated. Worse still, maybe he hadn't shown up at all, and *wouldn't* show, and I'd gone to all this trouble just to crash the kind of sex party that did nothing for me.

There were modest wet bars hugging opposite walls. I was about to order from the pretty little Latin bartender, who was in a black leather bikini outlined in silver studs, when I squinted through the smoky semi-darkness and realized who she was.

"Hiya, Gaita," I said to her. "What's a nice girl like you…? Skip it."

"I have been watching you." Her lush mouth was painted blood red, a moist glowing thing that surrounded her amused smile. "You do not stay long to look at the women as they play their games."

"Not my thing," I said. "I was worried about you, kid. I thought maybe Halaquez or his people had grabbed you."

She shook her head. She got me a beer without my asking for it, waited on another guest, and when we were alone again said, "No, this is just a job I took."

That was vague, but I didn't push it. "Gaita, is he here? Have you spotted him? Is Jaimie Halaquez here?"

But she was looking past me at something else.

Someone else.

"There she is, *señor*," she said. "The legend. The *living* legend."

I turned and at once I saw her…

…moving through the ballroom with regal grace, floating

like a ghost, and yet commanding attention and respect and even subservience, a dominatrix of stunning beauty and power, entirely in black, tall (but then those tightly-laced knee-high gladiator boots with the impossibly high heels contributed to the effect), in a latex gown, floor length but snapped open at the top of her sheer-dark-stockinged thighs, long black latex gloves almost to her bare shoulders, her face concealed by a mask that revealed little more than red lips and chin, with little devil horns, blonde hair spilling out onto her shoulders from under the mask.

The Consummata.

"Christ," I said admiringly. "She looks like the Catwoman in the old Batman funny books."

Gaita arched an eyebrow. "They say she has been around forever, *señor*. But does she look it? No. She is timeless. She is ageless."

Was Gaita making fun of me? There was something mocking in her tone. Or was there? With that ever-pounding, blaring grindhouse jazz, I couldn't tell.

My eyes were on the Consummata, who was moving slowly around her kingdom, legs flashing out of the floor-length gown, as she nodded to those subjects who dared to acknowledge her with a glance.

"Never mind her," I said, and turned my head halfway so Gaita could hear me. "Is *he* here, doll? Is Halaquez here?"

"He is," she said. Now her tone was cold. "Not long before you came in, his number came up."

"His number is up all right," I said. "Do you know which private room he's in?"

"No. Only the Consummata does. You will have to deal with her."

I shrugged. "You know what they say. You want something done, see the top man."

So I waited till our masked hostess had made her circuit and came near where I stood at the bar, and I stepped behind her. There was enough fog and smoke to conceal the fact that I was holding the point of a very sharp knife to the base of her back.

Because of her heels, we were on the same level when I leaned in to whisper: "Pain as fantasy is one thing, Connie. But you won't dig the real thing. Take me to Jaimie Halaquez ...*now*."

The hooded head nodded.

I couldn't walk behind her like that and not attract attention, so I fell in at her side. She knew I had the knife, which I palmed, and her sideways glance and the resulting up-tilt of her chin made me think she could sense I was truly dangerous.

So together we exited the ballroom, right past a security guy, and were in that hallway off of which the private sessions were conducted behind closed doors. None of the security staff spoke to her, but they all watched her close—she was clearly the boss.

Only the guy guarding the last door on the other end of the hall said anything, when the masked woman reached for the doorknob.

"Mistress," he said, and it sounded silly because he was another of the burr-headed Marine types, "you *do* know there is a session in progress."

She merely nodded, and went on in, and I followed her.

What we saw was the best tableau yet, and the only one that I found really entertaining.

In a fairly small room otherwise stripped bare, Jaimie Halaquez was on his knees on the carpeted floor, wearing only black latex skivvies, and his hands were cuffed behind him and a ball-gag was in his mouth. His back was red and bleeding here and there, laced with maybe a dozen slashes thanks to a thin-lashed metal-tipped whip in the hands of a black-corseted young woman with very short dark hair. She had spike heels and sheer dark stockings and the familiar trappings of the Consummata's craft. But like Gaita, she was a Latin girl.

Apparently Jaimie preferred to be beaten by his own kind.

He looked over his shoulder at us as the Consummata came in first, and swiveled around to gaze up at her like a praying man seeing a vision of the Madonna. He seemed delighted, seeing her, perhaps thinking he'd get special attention now from that fabled dominatrix.

He was half-right.

Then he saw me, and his eyes reflected a level of fear to which those play-acting girls in the ballroom could only aspire.

In her low, throaty tone, the Consummata said to her helper, "You may go," and the little Latin chick rolled up her whip and vamoosed.

I grabbed Halaquez by the arm and hauled him to his bare feet.

"I'm taking this clown with me," I said to my reluctant

hostess. "It can be messy, or you can walk us out, and nobody gets hurt who didn't pay to be."

Halaquez, that big bad man, was shaking like he was freezing. Suddenly being in handcuffs and ankle chains wasn't a good time.

The eyes in the mask holes narrowed, and the Consummata raised a "shush" finger to her lips. Without asking permission, she went to the door, cracked it open, and—before I could do a damn thing about it—she said, "Turn off machine number six. Right now."

The security guy out there said, "Yes, mistress."

She shut the door, turned to me and pulled off the mask. The blonde hair went with it, a wig that was part of the get-up. She shook her head and the dark hair fell into place.

And I got it.

I understood.

The Consummata was no one woman, rather a character used in the spy game by our side over the years to entrap sick bastards like Halaquez and to ensnare important people with kinks in their make-up who could be interrogated and blackmailed and generally manipulated, because the hidden cameras feeding video-tape ("Turn off machine number six") would provide the CIA with leverage the likes of which old J. Edgar Hoover himself might envy.

"I *told* you I was deep cover," Kim whispered.

CHAPTER THIRTEEN

"You could walk away," Kim said, "and let us handle Halaquez in our own way."

"What," I said, "and put this bastard back on the Company chessboard, to play more double-agent games? I intend to deliver him to the people he betrayed!"

Her gloved fists were on her latex-clad hips. "We have interrogators who make Consummata-type torture look like the playtime it is. We have truth-inducing drugs and deprivation techniques and psychological manipulation that can—"

"The only thing in this fucking skull worth knowing," I said, and slapped Halaquez alongside the head, "is the name of the traitor in the Little Havana ranks. And they will get that out of him, *and* deal with it, just fine. Trust me, my love."

There we stood in the bare little room, with the ball-gagged, handcuffed, very helpless Halaquez a mute witness to our little marital squabble, a husband with his knife and gun, a wife in her black bondage gown.

But she didn't argue any further.

"He's yours," Kim said. "Let them have him."

I had Halaquez's arm by one hand, but I took her arm by the other and grinned. "You look pretty damn good in black, doll."

And she grinned back at me, her mouth full and moist and red. "Do you like it? Then why don't you kiss me?"

I did. Hard and sweet and tender and rough, mashing my lips into hers with a fierceness that was anything but role play.

"Help me haul his ass out of here," I said.

"All right," she said, and pulled on the Consummata mask and again became the blonde dominatrix who ran things around here.

I tagged along as she dragged the whimpering Halaquez out into the corridor and down the wide stairway, and not a single security guy gave us even a second glance. We paused on the landing.

"I've got a boat waiting at the dock," I said.

Her eyes narrowed in the mask holes. "You understand I have to stay behind...."

"You need to do what you need to do," I said ambiguously, and she towed our quaking prisoner down the rest of the way.

Before long, we had moved through the downstairs and back through the kitchen, and outside where the night had grown a little chilly, wind riffling the palms.

Now we had the handcuffed, ankles-chained Halaquez between us, me with one arm, her with the other, dragging him along like the bag of garbage he was. He was trying to scream behind the ball-gag, but only a muffled grunting emerged, like something unpleasant on the tube with the volume way down.

As we moved along the row of gently swaying palms, he finally stopped his screaming, ceased any protest, his body slumping with despair, almost as if he were asleep or dead, and we had to tow him along. It slowed us, but not much.

When got to the dock, Saladar was still seated up in the

flybridge. He stood, his eyes wide and gleaming, his smile the same. Ever so slightly, he rocked with the motion of the moored craft.

"You have *done* it, *Señor* Morgan!"

"We've done it, Luis." We were almost close enough to the boat to step on board now, with Halaquez between us, like parents hauling a reluctant trick-or-treater to the next house. Kim stepped to one side to remove her mask, while I held our captive loosely by one arm.

"Luis, this is Kim, my wife," I said. "She's a government agent. Turns out this whole S & M set-up was an enormous sting."

Looking up at Saladar in the flybridge, Kim said, "You should know, sir, that you have the option of leaving this prisoner in my charge, for interrogation and maybe prosecution."

Halaquez straightened suddenly and his eyes were wide with something that was not fear, and I would have sworn he was trying to smile around that ball-gag. And was he laughing?

Could he be laughing...and why?

Saladar drew the .38 from his gunfighter's holster and shot Halaquez in the head, the report a whip crack that echoed off the water. The near-naked man in the black latex shorts went down in a pile on the dock leaving only a bloody mist behind.

Kim blurted, "What in the *hell*—"

I said nothing, my eyes meeting Saladar's. He lowered the gun but did not holster it.

"I am sorry, my friend," he said, bowing his head. He fumbled for words: "I am afraid...the emotion, it...seeing this traitor...forgive me...."

"I can't, Luis," I said.

His chin came up, his eyes implored me. "*Señor*...."

"*You're* the real traitor, aren't you, Luis? I suspected as much. I even thought you might try to kill Jaimie here on the voyage home, which would have confirmed it. But you didn't want to take that risk. You figured I might read the relief in his face when he saw *you*, the man he reported to...the man who has looted, manipulated, sold out, and betrayed his fellow Cubans in Little Havana, for how many years?"

The gun came up, though its snout pointed down at us from his perch. His sneering smile suited his devil's beard.

"I careened into Little Havana," I said, "and Pedro and the others embraced me as a possible savior. You played along, but betrayed me from the start. The very start. You were part of that small group, that first night, who knew of my masquerade, and knew I'd be at the Amherst Hotel."

He may have been a Commie, but his manner was imperial. "There is no need for this, *Señor* Morgan. You waste your words and your final moments. I am a soldier. I fight for a cause. You are a mercenary, the worst kind of capitalist."

If I distracted him enough, I might get to the .45. My suit coat hung open, after all. Then there was the knife sheathed on my left forearm.

Which could I get to faster?

"I wonder," I said. "Were you chasing Dick Best's nonexistent new invention for your *cause*? Or did you only see the wealth it promised?"

But I would never know the answer, because a second whip crack cut through the night and interrupted our conversation, a shot cutting through Saladar's shoulder in a blurt of blood, shoving him off balance, his .38 tumbling from his hand and plunking into the water like a stone.

Gaita stepped from the shadows and onto the dock, a striking, strange, barefoot vision in a metal-studded black bikini. She too had a .38, not a long-barreled one like Saladar had dropped in the bay, but a little police special that did the job just as well.

"*Ladron!*" she spat, and shot him in the chest.

Saladar teetered on the flybridge.

"*Asesino!*"

And shot him the stomach.

He lurched.

"*Traidor!*"

And shot him in the head.

Finally he tumbled.

Tumbled from the flybridge to the rear deck, and landed hard but surely didn't feel it, a limp rag of a human hitting with a thud that made the boat rock slightly, a death with none of the dignity he'd worn in life as part of his disguise.

Gaita came over to me and I held her. She was crying, but it seemed more anger than anything else. She started telling me how she'd seen Kim leave the ballroom with me, and how she had gone downstairs to wait to see if we would lead Halaquez out. The little avenger had been one of the girls hired by Kim to work tonight's affair. Bunny had been unaware, and...

I stopped her before she went into too much detail,

saying, "All I care about is that you're here, and that you shot that bastard."

Then I told her to go, and to take the gun with her, advising that she dispose of it.

"Tell Pedro everything!" I called.

"*Si, Señor* Morgan!"

She disappeared into the night.

Taking his wrists while I took his feet, Kim helped me swing Jaimie Halaquez's mostly naked corpse up and onto the rear deck of the *Black Beauty*, where he landed with a noisy thump next to the equally dead Saladar. We hadn't bothered discussing the obvious—that I would dump the bodies in the ocean.

The whip cracks had sent no one running down the backyard to see what the commotion was. Perhaps nobody heard anything over the blaring strip-club jazz. And the neighbors on either side were a world away.

"Come with me," I said to my wife. "I have this boat—it's mine now."

"You bought it?"

"Luis there sort of bequeathed it to me. And I have enough of a stake for us to get a good start on finding which of Sir Henry's hiding places holds the money-truck treasure."

We were on the dock, the wood spongy under our feet, standing down a ways from the bloody mess Halaquez had made. Nearby, on the rear deck of the craft, two corpses were sunning themselves in the dim moonlight. I had some blood spatter on me from Jaimie dying so nearby, and she had some on her black latex gown. Not as romantic a setting as I might have liked. Unusual, though....

"I have to stay," Kim told me, though the violet eyes revealed she hated saying it. "It's better if I clear you from the inside…. Someone's coming."

A single figure was running down the backyard toward us—not at a breakneck speed, just jogging, and alone. *One of the security guys?*

"I can handle whoever this is," I said.

"So can I. You have time to get on the boat and out of here…."

"Wait…it's Crowley."

"Morgan, go!"

"No. No, he and I have a truce. Didn't he tell you?"

"No! He didn't."

She and I hadn't talked since the fed and I had made our pact.

Then Crowley—in a dark suit that was similar to those of his agents up at the mansion, only better tailored—was on the dock with us. The breeze had picked up and was flapping his unbuttoned suit coat and ruffling his wispy amber hair. He glanced almost casually in the boat and saw the bodies there. Only a minor flinch registered on those bland features.

"So those *were* gunshots," he said to himself. Then to me, without a greeting, explained, "Guy on the door thought he heard gunfire down here. You do this?"

"No," I said. "A little Cuban girl who was working for you tonight. That's your incentive to keep the lid on."

"Oh," he sighed, rolling his eyes, "I *plan* to…. Are you all right, Miss Stacy?"

"Yes, sir."

"If you'll excuse me…." He moved away from us, down the dock, and used a walkie-talkie. He told somebody—presumably the man on the door—that there was no problem on the dock, but he would check out the grounds personally. No need for backup.

Then he came back and said to me, "You planning on dumping these dead fish?"

"I am. You have a better idea?"

"No. But I'm coming with you."

Kim pushed forward. "Walter, let's just walk away. Let Morgan deal with this. Don't you two have a truce?"

Crowley said, "A truce until the end of the mission."

"Actually," I said, "you promised me twenty-fours after I delivered Halaquez. Well, there he is."

"Morgan, I already *had* Halaquez, and you stole him out of my custody. Now he's dead and worthless as an intelligence resource. You violated our agreement. It's null and void. Now…here's what we're going to do."

And his small hand brought out the big nine millimeter from under his arm with admirable speed. I really hadn't anticipated it.

"Just a precaution," he said. "I can't send you out on that boat to dump those casualties without riding along. Miss Stacy, you come, too. Morgan, I promise you I will do everything I can to help clear you. But there'll be no getting away from me this time—and with Art Keefer gone, there's no one to come bail you out like after Nuevo Cadiz."

We got on the boat.

Up on the flybridge, I played captain and Kim sat next to me, and Crowley sat on the teakwood deck supervising the dead, hanging onto the rail with one hand and keeping the nine millimeter ready in the other. Not menacing about it or threatening, though he *had* asked me for my .45, which I'd handed over—it was in his waistband.

When the lights of Miami had disappeared behind us, and the ocean was an endless black ripple around us, touched with the barest shimmer of ivory from that slice of moon, I stopped the engines, and looked down at Crowley.

"Is this all right?"

"This will do," he said. "Come down, both of you, and give me a hand."

We did.

He held the gun on us as my wife in her black latex gown helped me take the corpses by their arms and legs and fling them into the drink. One at a time. The bodies floated, though as soon as the air in their lungs got replaced by water, they'd sink like stones; but right now they floated. And almost immediately I saw something chilling in the moonlight.

I pointed, and they both looked.

Nobody had to say it.

Fins.

Black fins cutting a white foamy path in the moonlight-touched blackness of the ocean.

For the first time, alarm registered in Crowley's voice. "Let's get the hell out of here." He motioned with the gun. "Back up there, you two."

In the flybridge in our side-by-side seats, I started the

engines up, and under their throbbing, Kim whispered: "He's the one, Morg. He's my suspect. And something he *said*...."

I whispered back, "I know."

I glanced back. Crowley was looking toward where the bodies had been floating, and sharks were now circling.

I called out: "Hey, Walter! Let me ask you something."

He turned toward us and frowned. "No small talk! Just get us back to that dock."

"Okay, let me ask Kim, then." I spoke to her but my eyes remained locked with his, and my voice loud. "Did you report in to Walter about Art Keefer's death? Is there any reason for him to know Art's name at all?"

"No," she said.

And I threw the knife.

It sank into his shoulder and, as part of his reaction, the gun in his hand went off, but luckily not at me or even at the teak-wood deck, just off into the night, echoing, bouncing, fading.

I leapt from the flybridge onto him, knocking him back against the rail, then yanked my .45 from his waistband and shoved it in his belly.

"Drop the piece, Walter. Let Davy Jones have it."

He did, and it barely made a splash.

Kim cut the engines. From her seat in the flybridge, she turned a grave, pitiless expression on him, looking more like the Consummata right now than my tender bride.

"That money-truck heist was a CIA black op," I said right into his terrified face, "and I was your patsy! You killed my friends, you've stolen years of my life!"

"You can't prove it!"

"I don't have to. I'm going out and I'll recover that missing forty mil, and turn it in, and all my sins will be forgiven. But it's something I have to do alone…well, almost alone. I'll have my wife with me."

That bland mug of his finally had some genuine expression, eyes wide, nostrils flared, upper lip curled back in trembling desperation. "You take me back, you can *have* your twenty-four hours! You can have forty-eight!"

"No, I'm going in another direction, Walter. And this?" I yanked my knife from his shoulder and blood plumed and burbled as he screamed.

"This is where you get off," I said, and shoved him over the back rail.

His screaming turned into a burbling thing and the white foam in the *Black Beauty*'s wake was red-tinged as he splashed and yelled and made a huge fuss. As I said, the moon wasn't providing much light.

But I could see the fins coming.

And so could he.

We lay anchor off a far key and didn't bother with swabbing the back deck of the blood of betrayers. That could wait. Right now we were celebrating our marriage with a couple of cold beers in the galley.

Sitting across from me, still in black latex, a wedding gown of sorts, she said, "What now?"

"Now we find that money. And when we find it, we can decide whether to clear my name or just spend the damn stuff."

"I can see how you'd figure you've earned it by now."

"That's right."

She nodded, once. "Okay. We'll go treasure hunting. We'll follow your namesake Sir Henry's footsteps around the Caribbean. But there's something else we need to do first."

"Yeah?"

And the Consummata rose, took off her long gloves before freeing herself from the black latex gown, letting it pool and clump on the teakwood floor, then propping first one foot, then the other, on the little galley table where I sat, as she unlaced and removed the high-heel boots, stripping off the black lingerie, nose-cone brassiere, silk panties, sheer stockings, garter belt, exposing full breasts, narrow waist, flared hips, long muscular legs, attributes that required no kinky accoutrements, all that lovely pale flesh interrupted only by the dark delta that, as she settled herself on the mattress of the forward berth, parted between creamy thighs to reveal the pink portal where life begins.

Those almond-shaped violet eyes taunted me.

"Don't you think," she asked, "it's about time we consummate this damn marriage?"

"Nag, nag, nag," I said.

**More Great Suspense
From the Authors of
THE CONSUMMATA!**

DEAD
STREET

by MICKEY SPILLANE

PREPARED FOR PUBLICATION BY
MAX ALLAN COLLINS

For 20 years, former NYPD cop Jack Stang has lived
with the memory of his girlfriend's death in an attempted
abduction. But what if she didn't actually die? What if
she somehow survived, but lost her sight, her memory,
and everything else she had...except her enemies?

Now Jack has a second chance to save the only woman
he ever loved—or to lose her for good.

**Read on for an excerpt
from DEAD STREET—
available now at your
favorite bookstore...**

It was quiet today. Overcast with a snap in the air. October was almost here and a fresh season of trouble was gearing up. Sergeant Davy Ross was standing beside an unmarked police vehicle, talking to a tall, thin guy in his fifties wearing black-frame glasses who had a white trench coat draped over his arm. In his hand was an inexpensive cardboard folder people keep receipts in and when Davy turned his head, glanced my way and said something, I knew they were talking about me.

Hell, I was the living anachronism, the old firehorse they couldn't get out of his stall, a dinosaur at fifty-six. Had to show up at home base the first of every month just to keep an eye on things.

Sergeant Ross grinned while we were shaking hands and said, "You got a fan from Staten Island, Jack. You remember that place?"

"Other side of the river, isn't it?"

"Roger. I think it still belongs to New York City, though." He paused and nodded toward the thin guy. "This is Dr. Thomas Brice."

When I took the doctor's hand, he said, "I'm a vet."

"What war?"

He grinned and the eyes behind the specs were alert and blue. "No, I mean I'm an animal doctor, Captain Stang. Don't want to get off on the wrong foot."

"No sweat," I told him. "I'm an animal lover myself."

Davy Ross cut in with, "You guys have your conversation. I'm going back to work."

We both told him so long and watched for a few seconds as he walked away.

When Dave went through the door, I said, "What's all this about, Doctor? You know, I'm not on the payroll anymore. I draw a pension."

Brice stared at me for a couple of seconds, his eyes reading me as though he were examining a strange breed of dog. It was an expression I had seen a lot of times before, but not from someone who didn't want to kill me.

Softly, Brice said, "Is there somewhere we can sit down? You must have a coffee shop around here somewhere."

I told him Billy's was down the avenue two blocks, an old cop's hangout that was about to go into the chopper when the station house shut its doors. Billy was finally going to have to go home and eat his wife's cooking for a change.

Two of the detectives from the other shift were winding up their tour and waved at me. Both of them eyed Thomas Brice with one of those cop glances that take in everything in a blink and they both had the shadow of a frown when they realized he was one of those clean civilian types and figured he probably was some distant relation of mine.

I winked and nodded back. They seemed relieved.

Over coffee and a bagel lathered with cream cheese, I said, "I haven't been to Staten Island since I was a kid." My eyes were cold and I scanned his face carefully.

"I understand," he told me.

"Neither do I remember ever having a case that involved that area."

His tongue ran over his lips lightly and his head bobbed again. "I know that too. I did some research on you and…"

"I'm clean," I interrupted.

"Yes, I know. You have a lot of commendations."

"A lot of scars, too."

I took a bite of the bagel and sipped at my coffee.

"It's a tough job, Captain," Brice said quietly.

"But nothing ever happened on Staten Island."

He was staring back at me now. I knew my eyes were growing colder.

"Captain, you're wrong," the doctor told me softly. "Something *did* happen on Staten Island."

I laid the bagel on the plate and under the table my fingers were interlaced, each hand telling the other not to reach for the gun on my belt. I didn't wear the shoulder holster with the old .45 Colt automatic snugged in it anymore. I was a civilian now. Still authorized by the state of New York to pack a firearm. But I wasn't on the Job anymore. *Caution,* I kept telling myself. *Easy. Play this hand carefully.*

Something was going down.

And the doctor was reading me. His hands stayed on the tabletop.

For several seconds his eyes watched mine, but they were encompassing every feature of my face. Then Dr. Thomas Brice broke the ice. It didn't tinkle like a dropped champagne glass—it crashed like a piece from a glacier. "Long time ago, you were in love with a woman named Bettie…"

A pair of tiny muscles twitched alongside my spine. It wasn't a new sensation at all. Twice before I had felt those insidious little squirms and both times I had been shot at right afterward.

He was saying, "She was abducted and stuffed into a van

but an alert had gone out minutes before and a police car was in pursuit. The chase led to the bridge over the Hudson River where the driver lost control, went through the guard-rails and over the fencing and fell a hundred and thirty feet into the water."

My hand was on the .45 now. My thumb flipped off the leather snap fastener and eased the hammer back. If this was a pathetic jokester he was about to die at this last punch line.

Softly, I said, "There was an immediate search party on the site. They located the wreckage. The driver was dead. There was no other body recovered."

The doctor's expression never changed, the eyes behind the lenses unblinking. He let a moment pass and told me, "Correct, Captain, no other *body*."

Something seemed to jab into my heart. I waited, my fore-finger curling around the trigger.

He added, "The next morning, right after dawn, one of the dogs in the cages at a veterinary clinic began whimpering strangely. It awakened the doctor—"

"A doctor named Brice?"

"Yes. But not this Brice—my late father. I was around, but not a vet yet. May I continue?"

I nodded.

"Anyway, my father got up to see what the trouble was. The animal was fine, but it was whimpering toward the rear lawn that bordered on the Hudson River. My father didn't quite know what was going on, but went with that dog's sen-sitivity and walked out the back."

Somehow, Dr. Brice read my expression. He knew that if

there was a downside to his story, he was never going to finish it....

"There was a young girl there. Alive."

Alive!

"One arm was gripped fiercely around an inflated inner tube."

He must have seen my arm move. Somehow he knew there was no tense finger around the hammer of a deadly .45 automatic any longer.

"The night before, we had heard about the altercation in the city, and we both knew at once that this girl was the one who had been abducted. The late news mentioned that it was a Mob snatch, as they called it, because sources within the NYPD indicated she had information that could seriously damage a major Mafia group."

"So you didn't report it," I stated.

"Fortunately not," he answered quickly. "My father checked with one of his friends on the local police force, who told him that the heat was on like never before and whatever that girl had could break up crime outfits from the city to Las Vegas."

"But nothing ever happened," I said. Something had rasped my voice. It sounded low and scratchy.

"Wouldn't have mattered," Brice told me.

"Why not?"

He let a few seconds pass before he said, "Because the girl...and she *was* a girl, twenty, twenty-one...had no memory at all of anything that had happened before the car crash."

And it was my turn to take a deep breath. "Nothing."

Dr. Brice shook his head.

I felt like vomiting. "Damn!"

"And that's not the only thing," he added.

"Oh?"

The eyes narrowed behind the lenses. "More than her memory was gone, Captain—she was blind. A terrible blow to her head had rendered her totally sightless. She would never be able to identify anybody…or be able to remember her past."

"So she was no threat to the Mob…."

"Come on, Captain. You know different. Until an identifiable body turned up, those people would never stop looking."

"That was more than twenty years ago," I reminded him.

Brice nodded slowly, his eyes on mine.

Before he could say anything, I let the words out slowly. *"Where is she?"*

He didn't tell me. He simply said, "That's why I'm here."

I knew there was a quiver in my voice when I asked, "Is she still alive?"

He nodded a *yes* and my pulse rate went up ten points.

She was alive! My Bettie was alive! I didn't care how she looked or how she remembered things, what she could see or couldn't see; my Bettie was alive and that's all that counted.

The old waitress came over, cleaned up what I had left of my bagel and refilled my coffee cup. I dropped in a couple of Sweet'N Lows and stirred them around. She squeezed my shoulder like she always did, and when she had walked away I asked the vet, *"Where*, Brice?"

"Safe," he told me.

"I didn't ask you that." There was an edge in my voice now.

"Can I finish the story?"

It was moving too damn slowly, but I wasn't leading the parade this time. It was his fifteen minutes of glory and, unless I wanted to risk slapping him around and losing his good will, I had to let him spell it out his way.

This is what he said:

"My father raised her. He nurtured her, cared for her in every way, educated her, made her self-sufficient in every manner imaginable. She was like a daughter to him."

"And a sister to you?"

Brice nodded. Then he leaned forward. "But there was always a little twitch in her memory, so to speak, that indicated she had a past somewhere. Not that it ever bothered anybody. In time even that went away."

"Did it?" I asked. "You're here now."

His smile was thinner than he was. "Very astute, Captain."

"Where *is* she?" I asked again.

"Safe," he said again.

"Where?"

"A prelude first…friend?"

"Make it quick. Friend."

"My father knew he was dying. The disease was incurable, but it gave him time to accomplish what he had to do."

"Oh?"

"His priority was to make sure Bettie was well taken care of. She had to be protected." He paused and added, "*Well* protected."

I nodded again, wondering where all this was leading.

He asked me, "Have you heard of Sunset Lodge in Florida?"

I bobbed my head quickly. "Sure."

He waited, wanting a further explanation.

"It's an SCS place."

When he scowled, I added, "Special Civil Service. A lot of the retired civil servants from the big city wind up their retirements there. Now they got the Jersey troops and the firemen in for neighbors."

"What else have you heard?" he asked me.

"Hell, they even have their own fire stations down there and the old cops are playing around with the kind of equipment we used to beg for. Man, the power of retirement voters."

"Florida loves them," Brice told me. "The cops all carry badges, legal but generously given, have permits to carry weapons; the firemen have all the best equipment and a real playground to spend their retirement years in."

"Who pays for all this?"

He didn't tell me. He simply said, "You'd be surprised."

We stared at each other across the table.

I finally said, "And she's *there*."

Crazy as it sounded, I knew what he was telling me was the truth and small shivers were beginning to run up my back.

She was alive…!

Pick up a copy of DEAD STREET today!